The Embers of Ravensforge

The Embers of Ravensforge

Book 2 of
The Children of Auberon

A Modern Faerie Tale
by J. Wolf Scott

For Mrs. Huffman
Blessings on your journey!
J. Wolf Scott
3/30/18

Printed in the United States of America
ISBN-13:9781479252121
ISBN-10: 1479252123

http://jwolfscott.com

For Rachel & Caleb

A Word of Thanks

To my amazing family, who puts up with the lack of time I spend cooking and cleaning as they tolerate my writing binges. Without your love and support, none of this would have been possible. You let me keep chasing this dream and going where the fae may lead from day to day, and I am eternally grateful.

To my friends who listen to me chatter like a magpie about faeries and pixies and hunting dragons and swords.....thank you for treating me like I'm somewhat normal. It's appreciated more than you'll ever know.

And to the folks at Minnetrista, who let me keep coming back, week after week, to haunt Oakhurst Gardens and search for continued inspiration: none of *The Ravensforge Trilogy* would have happened without your support.

And last, but not least, to my friend and editor, Sally Taylor, without whom this would be nothing more than a poorly punctuated, rambling mish-mash. She is truly worth her weight in gold. (Though she is quite diminutive in size, I still would not be able to afford her, what with the price of gold these days!)

With all these good folk around me, I count myself as one who is truly, truly blessed.

~ Julie

Prologue

His back against the wall, the prisoner shifted in the darkness of the cell. The stench of rot and decay hung thick in the air around him, making it difficult to breathe. At this point, he didn't much care.

His steel-blue eyes opened, wincing at the pain in the side of his head. Dried blood from his last three sessions with the minions mingled with the sweat of his brow, leaving ruddy streaks down his face. He closed his eyes again, letting his head drop back against the cold, stone wall as he reminded himself that there was only one thing he knew for certain.

They would come for him again. *Soon.*

They would come for him again, and when they were finished, they would eventually turn him over to the most ruthless enemy his kingdom had ever known. A malevolent being of immense power, consummate in the practice of cruel, dark magic; one who had been nothing more to him than a

1

figure of folklore known throughout the realm, nothing more than a scary bedtime story told to them as children in the Castle Ravensforge.

Castle Ravensforge.

All was lost that night at Ravensforge. Those he protected, those he had sworn his oath to, all those whom he had loved...*gone.* And he wished he were gone, too.

He could hear them coming. Claws on the stone floors, their guttural chatter back and forth amongst themselves that only they seemed to understand – *they were coming.* He could hear shuffling of other prisoners on the floors in the cells around him as they scurried back against the walls, but he knew they were coming for him.

The key rattled in the lock on the door of his cell and he took in a quiet breath, held it, then slowly let it out and opened his eyes. The heavy steel door swung open with a groan that echoed through the cell block as the minions swarmed his cell.

He did not offer any resistance, for he had nothing left in him with which to fight. They yanked him to his feet and half-carried, half-dragged him through the bowels of Erebos.

But this time was different.

Up a long flight of stairs that rose out of the ground before it wound around and around within a blue glass tower that looked as though it might have been a beautiful place at one time. But now it was filled with darkness, and an evil, unearthly glow that sent chills through even the bravest of warriors.

Pulling him to the top, they jerked him about like a ragdoll between them before continuing the last stretch of corridor to the throne room. The doorway faced them like a voracious, gaping maw waiting to devour all who entered there.

They dragged him across a decorative grate in the floor, dropping him in a crumpled heap before the throne of the Dark Warrior of Erebos.

The Warrior rose, his black, soulless eyes glistening in the waning light. Descending the steps, he deliberately took his time, circling as he sized up this heaving remnant of the Guard.

The prisoner remained atop the grate, its scrollwork digging deep impressions in his legs under his weight. His eyes adjusting to the blackness of the pit beneath him, he thought he saw something shifting about. *Something big.* He dared not move for fear of drawing its attention upwards at him.

Then again, perhaps that would be the more merciful of his options.

"I am in need of something you possess," the Dark Warrior said in a low, steady voice.

"What could I possibly have that you want?" the prisoner asked, his voice barely audible.

"The key to power over the realms," the Warrior replied. "I know who holds it, and you will tell me where she has taken it."

The prisoner's mind raced as fear washed over him like a giant wave. There was nothing the Dark Warrior could do to him that would be of any consequence. But in his realization of whom the Warrior sought, he knew he had to protect her at all costs.

He felt himself rise to his feet through no effort of his own or anyone else for that matter. He finally opened his eyes, the face of his captor a short distance from his own. His eyes were unnerving. *Hypnotic.*

The Warrior's black eyes grew wide as he reached into the prisoner's mind. A smile crossed his face as he read his captive's deepest thoughts. "You *care* for her," he said in a low tone.

Raising a hand, he twisted it and the prisoner began to see her in his mind's eye, and he fought the Warrior's influence but it was no use. It was as if he were no longer the only one in his mind. It was as if the Warrior had brought his cold presence into his very soul.

He could see her, sense the danger around her, and knew there was nothing he could do about it. He shook his head trying to clear the images from his mind.

"She is in danger," the Dark Warrior told him, "and only you can save her."

The prisoner could do nothing but stand there, wide-eyed, and take it all in, moment after pain-filled moment.

"Now," the Warrior said finally, his tone menacing and low, "you will tell me everything I want to know."

ಌ   ೞ

The trip back to the cell was a blur. The prisoner's mind was blank, conscious but aware of nothing until he was back in the underbelly of Erebos. He saw faces of others filled with fear and pity for him, and thought for a moment he recognized one or two of them. At this point it really didn't matter. The Dark Warrior would come for them, too.

The minions opened the cell door and threw him back in where they had found him. He welcomed the cold, stone floor against his face as he lie there hoping this would be the last time, but knowing it wouldn't.

Time passed and the cell door creaked open.

They had come for him again. So soon?

The prisoner pushed himself across the floor as if he would be able to resist, knowing full well he could not.

But this time was different. The minions threw another in the cell with him, screeching and snarling amongst themselves as they did so, then closed the door with a resounding clang.

The prisoner opened his eyes looking up at the newest resident of the cellblock. In the darkness he could make out a silhouette, nothing more. It was a long moment before the newcomer spoke words the prisoner needed to hear.

"We must escape this place," the stranger said, "and I know the way out."

Oakhurst
Enchanted

Chapter 1

Shea ran down the boulevard as fast as she could. She was already late and having to take the time to clean up wouldn't help matters any. Racing along the bike path, she cut across the narrow street and rushed through the gates of Oakhurst to the side porch. She hit the top in two steps and fumbled a bit with her keys before letting herself into the house.

She loved coming home to the big, empty mansion. It was quiet, and she rather liked it that way. Clambering up the back steps, she let herself into her tiny apartment. She fumbled through the chiffarobe, looking for just the right outfit – a floral sundress that she'd found downtown just days before.

She bumped her sword that hung from her belt on a peg inside the makeshift closet. "Won't be needing you tonight," she noted with a smile, as she closed the door.

A quick shower followed by the dress and a smoothing down of her hair, and she was ready. Grabbing a small purse and her keys, she bounded down the front stairs and let herself out the big wooden door and settled in on the steps of the porch as if she'd been waiting there all day.

Almost on cue, Connor came up the boulevard from Wheeling Avenue. Dressed in a suit, he looked quite dapper, and Shea smiled. Seeming to sense her eyes upon him, he looked up and couldn't help but smile back.

"Been waiting long?" he asked, as he came in through the gate.

"Only forever," Shea teased, "but I'd have waited longer if I'd had to."

ᔕ   ᣥ

Caeden made his way toward the fox's den. Chances were good he would find it occupied, but he had no other choice. The deed had to be done on this evening for the games would begin the next day, and it would be such a disappointment if all did not go according to custom.

His sword hung at his side and on his other hip, a pouch carrying his prize. It was relatively small but surely would not be missed by those who sought it. He was actually quite surprised that the council had asked him to handle this time-honored task. His dismissal from the Guard had been somewhat ill-regarded, in spite of the fact he had followed his royal charge's commands to the letter and had served with distinction.

He smiled to himself as he came upon the den. Three summers prior he had competed in the games, and his success had won him the honor of serving as Royal Guard to Prince Connor of Oakhurst. The fact that he looked like he was the prince's brother didn't hurt matters either, and he had served with pride until the very end.

Unfortunately, there was no need for him to serve in that capacity now, for Connor was living in the realm of the humans. Still prince of Oakhurst, but hardly needing protection from a fae, Connor was now more capable of protecting himself than Caeden would ever be.

Besides, there was Shea to serve in that capacity should the need arise.

Caeden had been relieved of duty following Connor's striking a deal with the one-eyed troll and subsequent passage to the human realm by way of the troll's dark magic. It could have gone horribly wrong, and Caeden wasn't sure if Connor truly understood the ramifications of what might have happened to him had it not worked. To this day, Connor could not return to the fae realm because of the dark magic, but still the queen hoped for a miracle.

Caeden peered into the den and was surprised to find it empty. Thankfully, this would be an easier job than he had previously thought. He eased his way into the hole and took the pouch from his belt, uncinching the cording at the top. He carefully took out the prize – a golden statue in the likeness of King Tamaran, just a little more than two hands tall.

The tradition was generations old, and the Games of Tamaran came around every three summers, usually toward the end. Named for Tamaran of Oakhurst, ancestor to Queen Liliana four generations before, he was known to this day as a wise king who took great pride in his Guard.

11

Legend had it that King Tamaran had been out in the garden hunting with the Royal Guard when he was snatched up by a red fox and carried off to her den to become food for her litter. Knowing their king would be set aside in the den for the sleeping pups to practice hunting with, the Guard had precious little time to rescue him. They ran swiftly to keep up with the fox and used all their cunning and stealth to rescue the king.

They were, of course, successful, and to reward them, the king vowed that his people would remember their deeds always.

Caeden placed the statue of King Tamaran in the farthest nook of the den and turned to go. In the dim light he looked about, noting that the den appeared as though it had seen a litter of pups a good while back, but he guessed they were a little older.

Crawling out of the den, he wrapped the pouch around his belt and began to walk through the undergrowth, taking the shortcut back to the palace.

Caeden startled, hearing the sudden snort a short ways behind him. He drew his sword and wheeled about to find a young fox rooting through the groundcover and moving toward him rapidly. Knowing it would not end well for him, he took the course of action that offered him the best odds. *He ran!*

The young fox, surprised at the sudden motion in the vegetation, let out a pup-ish *yip!* and gave chase. It barreled through the groundcover as it tried to corner Caeden and batted at him with its paws as much out of play as trying to secure a snack.

Caeden jumped and dodged and did his best to stay ahead of the kit, but he suddenly became aware of the fact that they weren't alone. Skidding to a halt, he looked up to find three more young kits staring at him.

"Oh, this is not good," he muttered to himself, as he looked round for a way out of this mess. How in the realm would it look if the last champion of the Games of Tamaran were eaten by the one thing he'd been sent to outfox?

Seeing no easy solution, he took the only option left to him – *he bluffed.* Sword raised high, he yelled at the top of his lungs and ran straight at the one that had started this whole game. Startled, the young fox jumped straight up into the air, his white socks easily clearing the top of the ground cover.

Caeden rushed underneath him just clearing his feet before they came crashing down again. The three other kits tried to follow him and ended up bowling the first one over. Distracted by the newest game at hand, they tussled and nipped and jumped on one another in the sunshine.

Returning his sword to its sheath, Caeden laughed as he ran down the path. Winning the Games had been easier than this! He only hoped that tomorrow's winner would have better luck with their new station than he had.

Rounding the fence post and ready to take flight, he was nearly knocked flat by three of the Royal Guard that stood at the base of the tree. Still breathing hard, Caeden tried to straighten himself out a bit. He hadn't been with them for awhile, had been avoiding them really, and even this was awkward at best.

"Hullo," Caeden said with a nod.

Stalwart and stone-still they stood there, arms at their sides and with one hand resting on their weapons. Finally, one of them spoke.

"Master Arland will see you at once."

        ঙ   ন্ত

Shea and Connor sat at a table just outside a lovely upscale restaurant down on Walnut Street. It was warm but not terribly uncomfortable, and the street was surprisingly busy with pedestrian traffic as folks walked along in the waning light of the day.

The waiter brought a bottle of wine and opened it, pouring them each a glass, then placed the cork back in the bottle and set it on the table. "Your dinner will be along shortly," he said. "Will there be anything else?"

"No, thank you," Connor replied, as he handed Shea a glass of wine. He rather relished the human realm and had grown to understand why it was that some fae, after crossing over, chose to remain.

He watched her as she looked at the people on the street. She was lovely, and he had known from the moment he first saw her in the Great Hall of Ravensforge that she was as beautiful and strong on the inside as she was outwardly.

Unfortunately, other matters competed for the attention of his mind, and he struggled with exactly what to tell Shea and what to keep from her until another point in time. It could greatly complicate the situation on several different levels, and Connor wasn't even sure if he had sorted it all out at this point.

His mother had informed him just that morning that one of the detachments had found a possible solution to his conundrum of returning to the fae realm…to Oakhurst. Of course, that would bring its own parcel of problems with it, but he wasn't willing to dwell on it tonight.

"What are we celebrating?" Shea asked, as she raised the glass, sniffing the wine as she rolled it around in the glass.

"The end of summer," Connor said, raising his glass as she followed suit, "and the coming of the Games of Tamaran."

"The Games of what?" she asked, after a sampling of the wine. It was a heavy red, and its flavor had caught her somewhat by surprise. She made a bit of a face and Connor laughed.

"Not what, who. King Tamaran is an ancestor of my family. It is how we bring new candidates into the elite ranks of the Royal Guard."

"Kind of like the Winter Ball at Ravensforge," Shea said fondly, remembering her own installation in the Guard. It was several seasons before she was assigned as Guardian to the daughters of Beltran. "We received our swords then. My father was so proud." She looked away, taking a moment to rein in her emotions, grateful that Connor was so understanding.

"I am anxious to see these Games," she said finally. "When do they begin?"

"Tomorrow," Connor answered.

His news of the solution could wait until then. It might very well complicate things. Tonight, Connor vowed to himself, would be only about them. No kingdom to rule, no royal obligations, no one to answer to or be responsible for.

Tomorrow would come soon enough, and when he told her, everything would change.

ᛒ   ᚳ

His pride still smarting from his failed attempt to protect his royal charge a season prior, Caeden stood humbly before Arland. Though certain that Connor would argue in his defense before the queen and the Master of the Guard, he knew he had no logical defense for his lack of action. At this point, he knew he would be lucky to be allowed to scrub the floors of the dungeon of Oakhurst.

Arland let the younger fae stew a bit before he spoke. His tone was controlled yet firm, and Caeden knew he was fortunate.

"The queen has an assignment for you," Arland said finally.

"Master Arland, I –" Caeden began, feeling the need to offer some explanation or, at the very least, an apology for the fifth time. He had been gone from the palace a good while now, just long enough to make things awkward between him and his mentor.

Arland raised his hand silencing Caeden. "Please, another apology will not be necessary."

"Yes, Master Arland."

"The queen has an assignment for you," Arland began again, "and it will be something you are already used to."

"I'm listening."

"She wants you to follow the prince."

Caeden looked somewhat confused. "Follow him?"

"Follow him."

"But he is a human now. How can I possibly protect him?"

"That is not what the queen has asked of you," Arland corrected him.

"I don't under–"

"She wants you to follow him and report back to her on a regular basis."

"To spy on him?" Caeden clarified, his eyes narrowing. "She wants me to spy on Connor? Why?"

Arland raised an eyebrow, and Caeden knew he had asked one question too many.

"I serve, as always, at the pleasure of the queen," Caeden said, as he lowered his eyes.

"I am counting on that, Caeden," Arland said. "And so is she."

CHAPTER 2

*"**People of Oakhurst,** I welcome you to the Games of Tamaran!"* Queen Liliana announced, to the cheers of the ocean of fae before her. On a branch above them, she delivered her royal decree. "My ancestor, King Tamaran, knew the importance of a strong Royal Guard and took great pride in their cunning and skill. Oakhurst has been a mighty kingdom for generations because of his wisdom, and today we celebrate those who wish to join the ranks of the elite warrior class."

On the next branch down stood six young fae, five males and one female. All appeared fit and strong, and though they stood before the entire kingdom, they acted as if they'd done it all their lives. None appeared anxious, and it would serve them well should they secure a position with the elite of the Guard.

They had already received preliminary training from Tristan, the training officer, as part of a larger class of hopefuls. Regular spot inspections by Arland, Master of the Guard, served to bring them up to the high standard as was demanded by Queen Liliana much more quickly than if they had been left to their own devices.

It was an honor to serve in the queen's Guard, and this year's winner of the Games would replace Princess Verena's Guardian. It seemed he had lost favor with the princess just prior to the loss of Prince Royce of Nebosham, and the queen had banished him from the palace immediately.

Master Arland stepped up and introduced each of the candidates: brothers Torin and Finnian, Gage, Parker, Keane, and Rayne.

"Each stage of the competition eliminates candidates. The first event is a footrace around the perimeter of Oakhurst Gardens," Arland instructed them, as he walked the length of the candidates' row. "The top five will continue on. The second contest, one of strength and stamina, will knock another from your ranks. The third and final stage, that of testing your mettle and courage, will involve only four of you."

Arland stopped, looking at them, his tone deadly serious. "With any luck, you'll all make it back."

ᛞ   ᚲ

The two sprites were up to no good, and though they could hear the roar of the fae crowd, they knew they had a job to do and had to finish it fast. If it played out according to plan, they would be able to watch it all unfold to its pathetic end, ruining the celebration of Queen Liliana's family tradition.

Carefully the pair crept into the fox's den. It was late in the afternoon, and the mother fox had taken her kits hunting. It was dimly lit, but it didn't take long for them to find what they were looking for.

There, against the back wall of the den, leaned the golden statue of King Tamaran.

Silently the pair snatched it up and bolted out of the hole in the ground hell bent for leather. They laughed with glee as they fled along the wrought-iron fence on the property's border. Knowing they couldn't stay on that path for long because the racers would soon be heading their way, they ducked into a hollow log to wait it out.

From there, the vantage point was spectacular, and they would have plenty to report back to King Rogan's court.

ဆာ   ၆

The candidates stood at the ready, awaiting the starter's signal.

"Runners, take your mark," Tristan shouted, his arm raised high above his head, "and.....*GO!*"

Keane took off like a bolt, streaking to the front of the pack as the others fell in. It would be a long run, and they were satisfied to let Keane wear himself out early. That way they wouldn't have to work quite as hard later on.

"Would you have wanted to compete again?" Shea asked Connor, once the runners were out of view.

"I don't know," he said wistfully. "Maybe. Then again, Mother probably would have said no."

"You don't always listen to your mother," Shea reminded him playfully. "Isn't that how you got here?"

"Yes, well, I had a very good reason."

Connor smiled as he leaned in and kissed her. For a moment the garden was silent, and it was almost as if they were actually human, unable to see the thousand fae that surrounded them.

It was the sudden concerted gasp that brought them to their senses. Shea and Connor opened their eyes to find all eyes in the Kingdom of Oakhurst focused directly upon them.

And one pair of eyes could have most likely burned holes straight through Shea.

Those would be the eyes of Queen Liliana.

               ᛒ   ᘔ

Caeden groaned inwardly as he watched the prince and the Guardian and the spectacle they made before the entire kingdom. The queen would be most unhappy with that, and he felt pretty sure he needn't bother with this report. The mass reaction from the crowd told him that she probably already knew.

Though his duty was to report directly to the queen, Caeden felt as if he were breaking a sacred trust between himself and Prince Connor. It was that trust that had allowed him to effectively defend the prince, if only through acting as his decoy on more than one occasion. At any rate, this did not bode well for any of them, least of all Shea.

It was one thing for the prince to choose a mate from royal stock and choose poorly. But to take up with the more common stock of the Guard, even though closer to royal

22

station than most commoners, it was still a post of service and would remain as such always.

And that was the only reason Caeden could continue with his mission from the queen.

~ ⊙ ~

The runners were nearly three-quarters of the way around the fenced perimeter of Oakhurst Gardens. All had managed to keep the ranks pretty tight, and it would be a close finish, but the last stretch was where it would get tough. And competitive.

From the middle of the pack Rayne saw them – two sprites making their way across the path and into the groundcover to parts unknown. She was somewhat surprised at their presence, and made a mental note of it to report to Tristan upon their return. Probably nothing, but being of a suspicious nature, she couldn't just let it go.

A trait that will serve you well, Master Arland had told her. *You will do well to hold onto it.*

~ ⊙ ~

"I miss this," Connor sighed quietly, as he and Shea waited for the candidates to complete the foot race.

The pair was seated on the grass in the formal garden near the finish line. The faeries of Oakhurst milled about them, and Queen Liliana sat upon a throne on a branch above as she observed the festivities.

"The one time I did compete, it was a coming of age of sorts."

"Really?" Shea asked, sounding a little surprised. "How did that turn out?"

"I did quite well, actually. I finished first but was disqualified."

"Disqualified? Why?"

He looked at her with a mischievous grin. "Well, it would be kind of hard to guard myself. I'd never get anything done."

Shea giggled at him, giving him a nudge with her shoulder.

Looking up she saw a young family walking the path through the arbor and headed their way.

"Act normal," Shea told Connor in hushed tones, as she smiled and nodded to the family. They returned the smile and waved as the children darted across the well-manicured lawn.

Unseen by human eyes the fae folk screamed and scattered as the children ran willy-nilly about on the grass.

One thing was for certain: it didn't add anything to the dignity of the games.

"Oh, look! Here they come!" Shea cried, as the runners rounded the hairpin turn at the end of Aunt Emma's path and headed across the grassy open space of the formal garden. She marveled at how they had all managed to stay in a pack to the very end.

All six of them turned up the speed and sprinted all out to the very end, with Torin finishing first, followed by Finn, Keane, Rayne, Parker, and finally, Gage. Breathing heavily, yet not fully taxed, all stepped over and bid Gage farewell. Gage, in turn, stepped before Tristan, bowed, and took a seat.

The remaining candidates moved on to the next stage.

ॐ   �

When all had settled down again, Tristan gathered the five remaining candidates together to give them their final instructions for the second stage of the Games.

All were charged with carrying a good amount of weight with them through an obstacle course. The candidates would work together to move a pile of bags filled with sand to a raised platform at the other end of the lawn. Meanwhile, senior members of the Guard would steal the bags and move them to other places for them to have to find.

In spite of the near exhaustion that plagued them, Rayne, Keane, Torin, Parker, and Finn made ready to complete the strength challenge.

"Because you never know what you will be called to do," Tristan informed them as he spoke to the crowd as well, "you must be prepared for any challenge, physical or otherwise." He looked from one to the other as five of the guards came before them. Each held a strip of thick purple cloth.

"You must complete this next task blindfolded."

"Blindfolded?" Shea whispered, as she leaned into Connor.

"Oh, this is the fun part," he answered back slyly.

Tristan watched as each of the guards tied the blindfolds around the candidates' heads, securing them with a double knot. At the sound of the whistle, all of them reached down to the pile of sacks and grabbed up one in each hand. Running toward their respective coaches at the other end, they lugged them to the other end and hefted them upward onto a shelf.

Though Finn had the upper body strength that Rayne was somewhat lacking in, Rayne had him in speed. Torin and Keane seemed to sense where the others were, dodging as they went along. Parker seemed to struggle, and when he called to the others, they responded in ways that were helpful.

Dropping the sack in her left hand, Rayne heaved one bag up with both hands, then reached back down and hefted the second one up. Running for all she was worth, she moved effortlessly as if still guided by her eyes.

Finn chose to throw each sack upward one-armed, first one then the other, and wheeled about and ran headlong back toward the cheering crowd. He was only a few steps from Rayne when she began her second trip. The other three candidates were hot on their heels.

Shea watched in amazement as they moved along, their eyesight darkened by the cloth coverings. She and Connor both sat in anxious silence, mostly out of respect for the candidates but also that it was not exactly prince-like to scream at the top of one's lungs at a sporting event.

Secretly, however, Shea was rooting for Rayne.

Finally, the whistle blew, and the candidates removed their blindfolds. All told, all of them had made it save Parker, who bowed before Tristan and took his place on the bench beside Gage.

CHAPTER 3

"My brothers and sister," Tristan began, as he addressed the candidates, "you have demonstrated great speed and strength thus far. But nothing separates the elite from the foot soldier more than the standard of courage and a sense of calm wisdom in the most rigorous of situations. This is what you seek in the third challenge even more so than the statue of Tamaran."

The fae of Oakhurst cheered at Tristan's words, and he waited a moment, both out of respect for their people but also to give his students an additional moment to catch their breath and get their heads together. One false move in this challenge could result in dire consequences at the mercy of the fox.

"King Tamaran was stolen away by a fox to be used as practice fodder for her kits...hardly a fitting end for a king. Our champion from the previous games has hidden it away securely in that very fox den that our great king had been held in so long ago." Tristan looked them up and down. "It is up to you to rescue his likeness."

With that, the four remaining candidates made ready to rescue the stand-in for their ancestor-king.

"Take your marks," Tristan shouted to them, "and...*GO!*"

Once again, the candidates were off at a dead run, headed straight for the Discovery Cabin. The fox's den was down a hole halfway between the cabin and the Colonnade Garden and was well-hidden to all but the most trained of eyes. Tristan had urged them all on more than one occasion to familiarize themselves with the entire grounds of Oakhurst, not just those around the palace. It would bring them a sense of peace as well as great success in the process.

Jockeying for position, they sprinted along the edge of the path toward the doll house. The groundhog that frequents the underneath space below the doll house poked his head out and offered up a guttural greeting as the foursome sprinted past.

Cutting through the undergrowth, Rayne decided it prudent to beat the others to the punch. She flung her arms about methodically as she raced across the wooded stretch toward her goal. The rest were nearly to the sprite home that the humans had placed in the garden two months prior before they realized she was even missing.

"Hey!" Finn called out. "Rayne knows a shortcut!"

"*Oiy!* Are you sure?" Torin answered back. "Could be she's just daft."

"Not bloody likely," Keane added breathlessly. "She's smart, that one."

Deciding to follow Rayne's lead, the remainder of the class raced headlong into the thicket.

28

First to the mouth of the fox's den, Rayne cautiously peered into the hole. The sun was sinking fast in the western sky, and she knew there would not be much time to waste. The prize was hers for the taking, if only she were brave enough to snatch it up.

A glance over her shoulder told her there wasn't much time. She could hear the three other candidates lumbering rather loudly through the brush, and she rolled her eyes wondering how they would ever survive in battle. Her hope was to never have the need to travel with them.

She sniffed at the air and could smell the musky scent of the fox. Listening for just a moment, she heard nothing and poked her head inside. Her eyes adjusted quickly to the lack of light. Cautiously, she stepped into the den.

Fox fur and pine needles lined the floor of the den, and Rayne quickly made her way in, feeling about for the statue. It would be dark soon, but the space was not that big at all, and she hoped to be out of there well before the others arrived.

Any sign of it would do, but a quick look about told her it was not to be found.

"Did you find it?" Torin asked somewhat loudly, poking his head in through the hole.

Perplexed, Rayne shook her head. "No, it's not here."

"Whaddaya mean it's not here?" Finn called in to her from just past Torin's shoulder.

"I mean it's gone," Rayne grumbled, as she climbed out of the den pushing her way past the brothers.

"Lemme see," Keane said, climbing into the den. "It's got to be here. Where else would it be?"

Torin and Finn both followed after Keane, peering into the den from just outside.

"Maybe it's a test," Rayne observed, as she moved in to look over their shoulders.

"She's right," Keane offered, poking his head out of the den. "It's not here."

Suddenly, Keane's eyes got large as saucers, and the others wheeled about to follow his gaze upward. Straight into the eyes of the mother fox.

ಲ   ಐ

From their vantage point near the fence, the sprites could hear the startled cries of the fae candidates as they scattered into the undergrowth. Theirs would be a feeble attempt to escape the mother fox and her kits.

"Too bad they've already eaten," the first sprite said, as he climbed up atop the hollow log to get a better look.

"*Aahhhh,* she'll just let them have at them a bit. You know, play with their food a little," the second said. "With any luck, they'll be snacks for later."

The pair laughed as they watched the candidates of the fae guard rush out from the groundcover and make a run for it. The four young kits scampered after them with their mother bringing up the rear.

With no weapons to defend themselves, the fae took the only course of action to them – they split up, heading in different directions in hopes that the foxes would follow suit. Torin headed deeper into the thicket. Finn doubled back on them, rushing straight at the one pursuing him and ran right beneath the kit. Keane had no choice but to run straight up the

30

brick path past the doll house. And Rayne bolted across the path and back into the woods.

It was then that she saw them – the two sprites perched upon the hollow log laughing at their peril. And below them lay the statue of King Tamaran!

Forgetting the fox for the moment, Rayne changed direction slightly running all the faster in their direction. Once in the groundcover the fox pursuing her stopped short, uncertain of where she had gone. Sniffing the ground, she began to root around in the weeds.

Seeing the opportunity, Rayne headed straight for the sprites. A short distance away, she bolted back out onto the grass, standing in eyesight between the fox and the sprites. Casting a glance over her shoulder at the sprites, she set her plan into action.

"Hey! Over here!" she called to the fox. "I've got something better for you over here!"

The young fox raised its head out of the vegetation and spied Rayne and the sprites. Rayne spun about and ran straight at them.

Shocked at her behavior, they had little choice but to flee. Rayne dove inside the hollowed out log and crawled as far in as she could as the pair screamed and ran in the other direction. The fox followed at a trot, bounding into the woods after them.

"Well, hello, Your Majesty," Rayne said, to the golden statue lying on its side next to her in the rather cramped space. "It would seem I have come to rescue you."

ᙦ   ᙟ

The candidates straggled back into the festival grounds exhausted. Torin, Finn, and Keane all looked as if they had been dragged through the grounds twice. They were covered in dirt and sweat, and their clothes were tattered from the chase.

"What has happened?" Tristan asked of them as they stood before him. "And where is Rayne?"

The three shook their heads, fearing the worst.

A sudden cry from the crowd brought Tristan's attention to the young girl-warrior as she emerged from the flower bed.

"Here I am," she smiled widely, the statue in her hands, "and I've brought along a friend."

ɞ

Rayne stood before Verena, Princess of Oakhurst. It had been a long day, and she had received her commission from the queen followed by instructions from both Tristan and Master Arland. She would become the princess's new Guardian, a post vacated by the last guard after an altercation with Prince Royce of Nebosham.

Unwilling to make the same mistakes, Rayne vowed to herself to learn all she could in this short period and serve with honor. And she knew that it would not be easy.

"Welcome, Rayne," Verena told her. "I am certain you will do well in your position. But know this: I am not one to be trifled with, and I know what is on your heart. I will not hesitate to dismiss you if I sense something is amiss. Is that understood?"

"Yes, Your Highness," Rayne responded.

"Good. The sooner we get that straight, the better off we'll both be."

ༀ   ༃

Connor and Shea sat on the front porch of Oakhurst enjoying the early evening as people occasionally strolled along the boulevard. Shea thought it somewhat funny that an entire major event had occurred earlier in the day in the formal gardens, and the humans were totally unaware that it had.

The Games had been exciting, and Shea knew that she would have enjoyed competing if she were still in the fae realm. She thought King Beltran would have loved the competitive nature of it and would have seen the Games as yet another way to showcase his Guard.

"Your Majesty," came a tiny voice from the other side of Connor. It was one of the queen's messengers.

"Oh, hello, Earlham," Connor said, as Shea leaned out so she could see the fae.

"The queen will see you now," he informed him, all business.

Connor sighed, as he looked at Shea. "Please tell her I will be there shortly."

"As you wish, Your Majesty," he said. "He has arrived."

Earlham nodded to Connor and Shea, then immediately took flight.

Shea looked perplexed. "Who has arrived?"

Connor cleared his throat. "Shea, I have something to tell you."

He looked at her a long moment, as if he were almost afraid to say what he had to say.

33

"My mother has found a way for me to return home."

ಶ   ೞ

Queen Liliana sat upon her throne in the back garden of Oakhurst and watched as Gregoir the Sorcerer unpacked his small bag of trinkets and potions on the table before him.

"How long does the procedure take to work?" she inquired, somewhat amazed at how much he had carried in with him.

"Oh, not long," Gregoir answered absently. "In my kingdom it has worked many, many times."

Queen Liliana's brow furrowed slightly. "Many times?" she echoed back, starting to wonder if this fellow was really someone she wanted to deal with. One of Arland's officers had vetted him, but his recommendation was beginning to seem suspect at best. Unfortunately, Liliana had reached the point of near-desperation and would give almost anything to have her son at home again.

"Yes, Your Majesty, many times," Gregoir confirmed. "It is guaranteed to remove all traces of the dark magic from his system."

"Let us hope you are right," the queen said. She looked up in time to find her son by her side.

"Hello, Mother," Connor said, as he knelt in the dewy grass next to the throne yet still towering over her.

The smile on her face told him everything – this was the solution they had been waiting for, and Connor came to it with mixed emotions. He had become comfortable as a human, enjoyed it even, and truly treasured every minute he'd spent with Shea. But all of that was about to change.

34

"Oh, Connor! So good to see you!" Liliana gushed. Then, in a more subdued tone, "Hello, Shea."

"Your Majesty," Shea said, with a slight bow of her head.

"Connor, I would like you to meet Gregoir the Sorcerer," Liliana said, as she presented the magician like a prize-winning 4-H project. "They tell me he is known throughout the realm for his miraculous cures."

"I see," Connor said with a nod. "I don't believe I've heard of him."

"I'm not surprised," Gregoir interjected. "It's hard to keep tabs on a sorcerer, you know."

"You travel a lot?" Shea asked.

"Oh, yes," Gregoir gushed. "Nearly been all around the world, fluent in many languages and travel in both realms."

He went on chatting as he mixed several vials of liquids together. They were each a different color, some glowing in the twilight. At one point a flash of fire and a puff of smoke exploded upward from the flask. Gregoir coughed and waved away the smoke with his hand, swirling the liquid with a twist of his wrist.

"There," he said proudly, "I think it's done."

He handed it up to Connor. The flask was tiny in his human hand, and he looked from Gregoir to his mother.

Queen Liliana nodded. Connor turned to Shea wanting to say something but found himself at a loss for words. He took her hand and smiled weakly as he raised the tiny flask to his lips and knocked back the glowing potion.

All watched expectantly as the elixir worked its way into Connor's system. After several minutes, Connor finally spoke.

"How long does it take?" he asked. "I don't feel any different."

"Wait for it, my boy," Gregoir told him, "wait for it..."

The sorcerer watched him, and the look on his face told them something was about to happen.

"...and, *now!*" Gregoir announced, pointing a finger at Connor. On cue the potion took its hold on the prince but not with the anticipated result. Instead of returning him to fae form, he began to change colors! His hair became a fiery orange, and his face a glorious shade of purple that any royal would have envied. His arms and shoulders glowed a brilliant greenish-yellow, while his torso was the lovliest shade of turquoise.

Queen Liliana gasped as her son transformed before her eyes from a human of normal tones to a walking, glowing rainbow. Shea dropped his hand, uncertain of what to do next. Astonished, she could only watch as the potion took effect.

"I don't feel different," Connor noted, as he looked at his hands as they shifted from one color to the next. He was starting to feel like a neon sign at this point.

"You sure *look* different," Shea told him with as straight a face as she could manage.

"Oh, my word," Gregoir muttered.

"Gregoir, this is not what we agreed upon," Queen Liliana hissed.

"Yes, well, sometimes these potions have a mind of their own...especially when you mix them with dark magic. We did discuss the possibility that it might not work, Your Highness."

Queen Liliana sighed in acknowledgement.

After a moment the colors faded, and Connor went back to being normal.

Human-normal.

CHAPTER 4

The council of Oakhurst was seated before the queen in her courtyard behind the house of Oakhurst. It was a late summer evening, and there was a stillness on the grounds in spite of the fact that the delegation from Nebosham was approaching.

Connor sat cross-legged on the cool grass to the right side of the throne, as he would if he were in his mother's court. Shea sat next to him, just about half a foot away from the council.

Momentarily the regent spoke up. "Your Majesty, may I present His Royal Highness, King Rogan of Nebosham."

Eyes forward, King Rogan approached the throne with a sense of bravado that Shea hadn't seen in a great while. It had been difficult for him since the loss of his son, Prince Royce. Shea empathized with him more than anyone – she had lost her entire family in the destruction of Ravensforge and witnessed his loss as well.

"King Rogan, I bid you welcome," Queen Liliana said with a nod. "Your arrival has been long awaited. What say you on the matter of the relics."

"She doesn't waste any time, does she?" Shea whispered to Connor, who said nothing in response.

Shea struggled with how she felt about the whole situation. She had been in possession of the relics since the incidents of Faeries, Sprites and Lights some months before, and felt better knowing their whereabouts instead of having them spread to the four winds, much less divided amongst the three remaining kingdoms. While the decision lay in the hands of the royals, Shea felt she should have some say in the fate of the relics for the simple fact that she was now the Guardian of Oakhurst and thus, Guardian over all the kingdoms of the fae realm. If the tools would protect the kingdoms most effectively in her hands, she would feel the need to speak up.

"I do not believe we are best served by leaving the relics in the hands of the Guardian," Rogan said in earnest. Though his posture seemed belligerent, his words did not. *Yet.*

"Whose hands should they be in?" Queen Liliana inquired, as she leaned in to emphasize her sparsely veiled point. "Yours?"

"Why not?" Rogan agreed. "If we are truly as equal as you treat us in your court, should we not have a say in the relics' fate? Even further, should we not have a stake in their holdings?"

"Explain," the queen said.

"Such great power – such faerie magic – should remain in the realm of fae and sprites, not humans. You know the dangers involved in crossovers. Such use of fae magic in the human realm could have disastrous results beyond our comprehension."

"There is the matter of returning them to the realm," Liliana said. "The portal was destroyed. And while there are others, they are a great distance away, both in the human realm and our own."

"There are other ways," Rogan replied.

Queen Liliana looked up at her son. *Oh, how she missed him!* She would do anything to get him back to the realm – to the throne where he belonged. But she knew that to do so would put his life *and* his reign in peril.

"What are you suggesting?" she inquired.

"I am merely stating that there are ways that have yet to be discussed that will allow the relics to once again be part of the fae realm where they belong," Rogan said pointedly, as he looked up toward Shea. "They do not belong in the hands of humans."

Shea took a deep breath remembering all Elisabeth had taught her as Guardian of Oakhurst. She hoped she could do half as good a job as her mentor but knew there was a learning curve to it.

"If it pleases Your Highness," Shea began slowly, "I would remind you that I am from the House of Beltran, loyal servant and Guardian to the daughters of the king. While I dwell in the land of humans, I am not truly one of them."

Rogan heard nothing past Shea's record of service. "Guardian to the daughters of the king, hmmm? Well, we saw how well that turned out, didn't we?"

Stunned, Shea hardly knew how to respond. She felt anger rising in her gut but knew well enough not to let it get the best of her. She could protest the council's decision or just ignore it altogether. What would they do? Try to steal relics that were much larger than Arland's strongest warrior could handle and awkward as blazes for even a dozen fae to attempt to haul off? Honestly, it was trying her patience.

The entire council sat as one in utter silence waiting for Shea to respond. Whether it was inexperience in the ways of diplomacy or simply the distance between their stations, she found she could only allow her silence to agree with him.

ᙚ   ᙖ

Verena sat among the branches just above the council. She could hear them but didn't really listen to what they were saying. She couldn't bear to be in attendance for the simple fact that every time she saw King Rogan of Nebosham her heart and arms ached for his son. Though only a few months had passed in the human realm since Royce had disappeared, it seemed like an eternity for Verena, and it was all she could do to function day to day.

Rayne stood watch a short distance away. Verena appreciated her new guard's intuitive nature, knowing when to be nearby and when to make herself nearly invisible. If Verena didn't have the gift of discernment, she would hardly know Rayne was even there.

Verena didn't envy Shea's position or role in the council's business. In spite of Elisabeth's fondness of her, Shea would soon learn that there is more to being the Guardian of Oakhurst than she could have possibly imagined. Her mother would see to that. Verena could see it in the queen's eyes every time she spoke of Shea in private. Decorum would never allow her to disrespect the Guardian in court or in talks with

Nebosham, but in her most unguarded moments, Queen Liliana was not afraid to speak her mind.

Verena did, however, envy Connor. And it wasn't that he was in the human realm, or even that he was freed – at least temporarily – of his royal duties. She envied the fact that he could be with the one he cared about. Though they had been unable to locate the princesses of Ravensforge, Verena thought it a little more than convenient for Shea that Connor had been so ready to simply give up.

Verena knew her brother well enough to know one thing: as Crown Prince of Oakhurst, next in line to the throne, Connor would never step away from that role willingly unless there was a very good reason.

And to his sister, it was as plain as day: Connor had a very good reason.

He was following his heart.

ಶು   ಅ

"Rogan is a fool," Shea blurted, once she and Connor were safely inside Oakhurst. They walked up the front stairs in silence and settled in on the sofa on the sleeping porch. A thunderstorm had rolled in, and the steady beat of the raindrops on the roof did little to soothe her as it usually did. She knew the fae did not like to be out in the treetops in the rain, so their conversation could be completely candid as long as the rain held out.

Connor shifted uncomfortably at her rather brash opinion. One did not simply disrespect the monarch of another kingdom without being prepared for repercussions.

"I am sure he has the best of intentions," Connor said

finally, trying to defend him.

"Good intentions and ninety-five cents will get you little more than a cup of coffee down at Jackie's diner," Shea scoffed.

Connor raised his eyebrows. "Since when did you become so cynical?"

Shea sighed heavily. "I'm sorry. I am simply...frustrated at the shortsightedness of Rogan, the council, the humans. These are powerful relics and, quite frankly, I don't know anything about them. Sure, the humans think they're 'cool,' but they also believe they belong in a museum collection. They don't fully understand what they are dealing with here."

"Neither do you, apparently."

"No, I don't," Shea agreed, "and that's what scares me."

CHAPTER 5

The smells of the diner greeted Shea as she opened the door to the downtown eatery. She had missed her friend, Jackie Robinson, and it had been far too long between visits. Jackie was her first friend from the day she came to Oakhurst, and today she was back to repay the favor.

"Hey, *faerie girl*, how you doin'?" Jackie greeted her warmly with a smile and a hug.

Shea smiled back at her. "I am well," she replied. "Are you ready for this?"

"I am, but I don't know about Paul!" Jackie quipped. "We've only got a couple of weeks 'til the wedding, and he will probably be working on the day of the wedding right up until the ceremony. Then he'll go help the catering staff in the kitchen!"

"A bit obsessive, is he?"

"Oh, *girl*, you have no idea."

ꕤ ꕤ

The two women walked down the street a few blocks, crossed over a parking lot and came out on Walnut street. They hung a right, then continued two more blocks to a small dress and bridal boutique in downtown Muncie.

Jackie's sister, Jenny, was already there with her young son, Jackson, in tow. Jenny hugged them both obviously excited at the intended reason for being there.

"Jackson, you be a good little man and wait here while Aunt Jackie goes to try on her wedding dress," Jackie told her nephew. "We'll go have lunch when we're done."

"Yes, Aunt Jackie," Jackson said, as he found a seat.

Shea, Jenny and the attendant made sure Jackie had everything she needed, then headed off to the dressing room themselves. Moments later both emerged in two different cuts of the same dress in a soft shade of pink.

Both looked lovely in them, but Jackie stole the show. She stepped out of the dressing room in the gown, veil and a tiara on top of her head, grinning from ear to ear. Her dark skin highlighted the crisp, white fabric and laces that flowed from just beneath her shoulders to nearly all the way to the floor.

"Well," Jackie beamed, "how do I look?"

Shea grinned. "Like a faerie princess."

ꕤ ꕤ

"Good day to you, Shea of Oakhurst," Queen Liliana greeted her formally. There was an icy edge to her voice, and

Shea knew to keep her place. "Have you gathered the information I have requested?"

The queen sat in her throne made of flowers and twigs high up in the branches of the tallest oak tree in the garden. Shea liked to think that the queen always asked to meet with her here because she liked the view, but the cynical side of her was convinced it was more out of the queen's desire for her to simply fall out of the tree and break her neck. That would be the easiest way to dispose of the girl-warrior who had captured her son's attention with her son being none the wiser. Then again, Shea had always been somewhat of a conspiracy theorist even in her days at Ravensforge. King Beltran had told her that was what made her so valuable to him.

"Of course, Your Highness," she answered politely. Then with a nod, "Hello, Arland."

As always, the queen's bodyguard was at her side, silent and resolute in his station. He smiled slightly and nodded. She admired him for his loyalty and steadfastness and could see in his eyes that it was something more for him than merely protecting Liliana, but that it would never go any further than that. Shea was sad for him, but held it in check for his was a keen eye and could read others nearly as well as Verena with her gift of discernment.

"The humans are progressing with the landscaping of the north end of the grounds with an anticipated completion of the project early next year. It should not interfere with the goings-on within your kingdom nor those of Nebosham."

"Estimated ecological impact?"

"Minimal."

"Disruption to our own efforts in preparation for winter?"

"Again, Your Highness, minimal."

45

"I see, very well. And concerning the matter of my ancestor's likeness being stolen during the games…do we have anything solid yet linking the two sprites to any serious conspiracy or threat?"

"No, Your Majesty, not yet. Master Arland has fae on the ground following a couple of leads, but there is nothing solid to report as of yet."

"In your opinion, Guardian," the queen inquired, "do you believe King Rogan was directly involved?"

"It is possible," Shea answered hesitantly, "but I prefer to withhold judgment on that until we have further evidence to substantiate our suspicions."

"Very well."

Though the news was not exactly what she wanted to hear, Queen Liliana appeared to Shea to be somewhat preoccupied by other things. She shifted in the throne and sat quietly a moment gathering her thoughts. When she spoke, her tone was cool and calculating. Her words nearly knocked Shea out of the tree.

"I have another mission for you to carry out," she said as she held Shea's gaze. "For the good of the Kingdom."

"Of course, Your Majesty," Shea responded obediently.

"I want you to get my son…oh, I'm sorry, what is the word? *Fired*," Queen Liliana said. "Yes, fired. I believe that is the word the humans use."

Stunned, Shea shook her head. "I'm sorry…what did you say?"

Not one who was used to having to repeat herself, the queen cleared her throat, then said again, "I want you to have the humans relieve Connor of his position."

"For what reason?"

"Come now, Shea, you are a bright girl. You are a well-trained warrior, and I am glad to have you as protector of our kingdom. But we both know that Connor was born for greater things than to be a – a *gardener* among humans."

Shea knew the queen was right. But she also knew that Queen Liliana was a skilled diplomat, one who knew the art of negotiation, and especially one who knew when to leave certain things unsaid. The queen's eyes locked with Shea's, and Shea knew exactly what was left unspoken.

It was Queen Liliana's belief that Shea and Connor could never be together.

And unfortunately, Shea found that she had to agree.

"It will take time, Your Majesty," she said quietly, eyes cast down at the ground some thirty feet below them.

"So long as it is done," the queen agreed. "Take your time, and I don't care how, but know that by the winter solstice it must be done."

ঙ   ও

Shea climbed down from the tree dumbfounded and utterly heartsick. She had grown fond of Connor – even more than that if the truth were told – and her feelings aside, she could not believe that his mother would ask her to do this.

His own mother!

Then again, she had been surprised at the importance King Beltran had placed upon the amulet he hung around her neck on the night they fled Ravensforge. Though it went unspoken between them, Shea knew that he deemed the safety of the amulet of greater import than that of his own daughters.

"For the good of the Kingdom," the queen had said.

Shea could fight it in her mind a thousand times over, but in the end she would always reach the same conclusion.

Queen Liliana was right.

Chapter 6

The remaining weeks flew by, and the wedding of Miss Jackie Robinson to Mr. Paul Harper was a joyous affair held in the Rose Garden on the south lawn at Minnetrista on a mild late-September day. The rest of Jackie's family had practically adopted Shea and treated her like one of their own.

The ceremony was beautiful, and Shea stood with Jenny next to Jackie as she and Paul said their vows, promising to love, honor, and cherish one another 'til death do they part.

Standing sideways, Shea caught a glimpse of Connor and found him watching her. She smiled at him, then turned back to the matter at hand.

Connor continued to watch only her. She was beautiful, and he found himself falling for her more and more each day. It was complicated, but he knew that if anyone could make it work out, they could.

The wedding party stayed up in the Rose Garden for pictures while the guests filed down the boulevard to the main gate of Oakhurst. A white tent was set up in the formal garden, and an elegant dinner awaited the bridal party and their guests followed by a string quartet and dancing. While it was not the conventional fare of the day so far as weddings go, Jackie had been inspired by Shea's new home and wanted her special day to be a little more of an old-fashioned sort of elegance.

The food was exceptional, and the quartet began to play as guests took to the makeshift dancefloor. Finally relieved of her bridesmaid duties, Shea set her flowers aside.

"Breathtaking. Simply breathtaking," Connor gushed, as he came up beside Shea.

"The wedding was gorgeous, wasn't it?" Shea agreed.

Connor smiled as he stroked her cheek. "I meant you," he said.

Shea blushed and stood there awkwardly, not sure what to say. It was Connor who broke the ice.

"May I have this dance, milady?"

"Why, I'd love to," she grinned. She felt a bit guilty, knowing what the queen expected of her, but at the same time she knew that she could at least enjoy this special occasion with Connor before winter came. She would put it off as long as possible. True, she was courting the queen's wrath, but Shea decided she would deal with that later.

"It was a beautiful wedding," Connor agreed finally, as he swept her around the dance floor. He smiled down at her, somewhat puzzled by the look on her face. "You seem surprised that I can dance," he teased.

Shea laughed. "I'm not sure why I expected any less. You are, after all, a prince. And the daughters of Beltran were

50

schooled in many things, including formal dance, so why wouldn't you be equally taught as well?"

Her expression clouded, and Connor could read it almost immediately. He had become rather good at that of late, and he enjoyed surprising her with it sometimes. Here, however, he knew he had to tread lightly.

"You are thinking of your charges, are you not?"

"Yes," she admitted. "If things had remained the same, you would be betrothed by now, and life would be very different."

"True," Connor replied, "but I am not unhappy with how things have turned out."

Connor knew that Shea struggled daily with her feelings of guilt over what had happened at Ravensforge and the subsequent loss of her royal charges and everyone she knew, for that matter. Her family, her friends, those whom she had protected and served, all were lost, and he could only imagine her pain. At least he could see and speak with his family whenever he chose. However, going home was not an option for him.

He knew his physiology had changed since the day of his arrival. It was the remnants of the dark magic, of that he was certain. He knew there would be grave consequences, most likely resulting in his demise should he return to the faerie realm. So to him, while the decision was no less difficult, remaining at Oakhurst in the human realm was what the humans referred to as a "no-brainer." And besides, if he were to be stuck somewhere, at Oakhurst with Shea is where he would choose to be.

He smiled at her as they continued to dance. "You know, my mother always sends a representative to weddings in the

51

garden," Connor said out of nowhere, as he glanced around. "There is probably one watching us right now."

"Oh, great," Shea replied, rolling her eyes. "I'm sure *that'll* go over well back in the council."

Connor laughed. "Oh, come now. You know she already gets reports on where I am and who I'm with on a regular basis. She would know that if I were fae sized…why would this be any different?"

"True," Shea answered, "but if we were both still fae, this would not be happening."

Connor leaned in, his lips close to Shea's ear. "Then I'm glad we're no longer fae," he whispered.

When he leaned back, Shea looked into his eyes and knew he spoke the truth.

৶   ໕

From across the garden Verena watched Connor and Shea as they danced and knew that her mother would be most displeased. Verena had volunteered to be the fae representative at this wedding knowing full well that Shea was involved. And while she wanted her brother to be happy, she was not sure this was the way it needed to be. She found herself agreeing with her mother, if only for the good of the kingdom and her brother.

Her heart still ached each time she thought of her beloved Royce and how he had sacrificed himself for all of them, for the good of the gardens. She could scarcely bring herself to speak his name, and though Queen Liliana hated the fact that Verena was in so much pain, she knew her mother preferred it that way.

Verena knew there was a history of bad blood between her mother and the sprites of Nebosham, but she did not fully understand why the queen held such contempt for them. She knew King Rogan was neither the most tactful nor the most politically savvy being in the realm, but truly, who among them on the court was?

Verena did sense that Shea was good of heart and honestly cared for Connor. And while that should ease her mind, the fact remained that Shea, even in her new post as Guardian of Oakhurst, was still not Connor's equal. Hers was a post of service and, if necessary, sacrifice. His was of leadership and regality, regardless of which realm he was in.

From the looks of things, he was enjoying the human realm just fine. And Verena had to admit that they really did make a fine-looking couple. They laughed and danced and talked most of the evening, and she could tell they were happy together.

A tear rolled down Verena's cheek as she watched them, knowing she would never have that with Royce. Though she held out a sliver of hope that he may still be alive somewhere, she knew that if she ever got him back, he would never be the same. Yet she wondered, *Did that really matter?*

The reception now over, Verena watched as Connor escorted Shea back to Oakhurst. They looked as if they belonged there together. She might be able to be happy for them, but she doubted very seriously that her mother would ever be able to accept it.

And that could cause problems.

ಬ   ಐ

Caeden had hidden himself away just above a flap in the top of the tent in the formal garden and had a bird's-eye view of the goings on at the wedding. From his vantage point he could see Connor clearly and knew that the queen would not find his report favorable.

The entire time they'd been under the tent, Connor had scarcely left Shea's side.

Caeden was fond of his royal charge and was secretly glad to see him happy but could also understand the queen's ire at the situation. The closest he could equate it to would be if he were to suddenly decide to court Verena, and he knew that the queen would never allow that to happen. Not that he wanted it to.

The problem with this situation was quite simple, really: Connor and Shea were too big for the queen or her Guard to do anything about it. There were, of course, those who speculated that Queen Liliana would resort to drastic measures, should the situation warrant such tactics as using dark magic. Caeden, however, was certain she would never stoop that low and hoped like hell he was right.

The last thing any of them needed was to mess with that.

Caeden looked down at the humans beneath him as Shea and Connor twirled around on the dance floor. They truly did make a nice-looking couple, and who was he to cause problems with that?

The prince's Guardian, he reminded himself, *sworn to protect him at all costs, including the wrath of Prince Connor himself.*

CHAPTER 7

The sun shone brightly through what was left of the leaves on the trees of Oakhurst. Fall was fading fast, and in spite of the queen's directive, Shea and Connor enjoyed their time together as much as possible. The humans of Minnetrista spoke often of snow and that winter would be here soon enough, so the pair enjoyed frequent picnics in the garden.

The air was crisp but neither of them seemed to mind. The damaged plant life from the dragon was recovering nicely, and the gardeners had assured Shea that it would be good as new come spring.

"Your mother seems a bit out of sorts these days," Shea told Connor, between bites of her sandwich. True, Liliana held her own in the council and had not spoken since of their conversation concerning what must happen with Connor. There was underlying tension between the two women in his life, and Shea was curious to see if he had noticed.

Connor smiled. "Well, that's really nothing new," he replied. "You just haven't known her long. Ruling a kingdom on your own is a big responsibility."

"I have no doubt that it is."

"She was anticipating preparing someone else for that role."

Shea looked down remembering the princesses of Ravensforge. They had been attempting to locate them since the faerie event a few months ago, but nothing had come up. She was somewhat frustrated in the lack of good leads but knew little would come of her fretting over it. Connor had put several of the Guard in his mother's court on the search, but thus far they had found very little to go on.

Sam Cooke had jokingly suggested that they put the princesses' photos on milk cartons, but when Shea had pointed out that there were no photographs of the pair to speak of and that any formal portraits had burned with Ravensforge, Sam just shook his head.

"You have fulfilled your duty, Shea," Connor told her. "We will find them, but for now, there is nothing more to do." He watched her noting a hint of sadness behind her eyes. "You have been called to something different now."

Shea smiled, trying to mask her true feelings. It was an awesome responsibility left to her by her dear friend, Elisabeth. Though she missed her terribly, Shea could still sense her presence in the garden and looked for her often. She was never there, of course, but still Shea took comfort in knowing that hints of her spirit still lingered there.

"And you as well, seeing as how you can no longer return to the realm."

"No higher calling than that of gardener," he teased. "Besides, I'm too big for the throne."

Shea shuddered in the knowledge that he was truly called to be much more than that. "Connor, would you like to go back?" she asked. "Would you return to the fae realm if given the chance?"

"The question is of no matter," he sighed. "I cannot return; therefore, I do not dwell on it. There is no point in being unhappy that I cannot go home. I can still see my mother, my sister, my friends, whenever I choose. I just cannot rule my kingdom." Connor reached out and took her hand. "Is that really so bad?"

"Still, the question begs asking."

"I am here," he replied, "and I am content."

Shea smiled at him, but her heart ached that his home was just out of reach. She remained secretly pleased, however, that he had adjusted so well. They both had, really, and Oakhurst was becoming more and more like home for them with each passing day. She dreaded the day when all that would come to an end...*at her hand, no less.*

Connor had rented a small flat in a house just across Wheeling Avenue, and they would often share meals together. They had made friends with some of the students in the neighborhood, and it was good getting to know people their "own age." Humans were a different lot, but Shea and Connor were both beginning to see why fae sometimes crossed over and decided to remain.

"Then, no," she added, "I suppose it could be worse."

"You have to admit," Connor said, "life is pretty good."

࿇   ࿇

"You have news for me, Caeden?" Queen Liliana asked, as her son's former Guardian entered the throne room.

Caeden swallowed hard, knowing that the queen would not be pleased. He had just come from the garden, had witnessed Connor and Shea sharing a moment and dreaded with all his being having to tell Connor's mother about it.

"Yes, My Queen," Caeden said, as he bowed low before her. He rose and looked her squarely in the eye knowing insolence was frowned upon in her court. "Prince Connor appears to be...*happy*."

Queen Liliana shifted in her throne. "Happy?"

"Yes, My Queen. Happy."

"And Shea? Is she happy as well?"

Caeden swallowed hard knowing it would not be the answer she wanted to hear.

"Shea appears to be happy as well."

Queen Liliana rose, stepping down from the throne and approached Caeden. Eyes lowered, he was contemplating his fate when the queen spoke.

"Very well, Guardian, that is all."

℞ ℟

It was late fall, and a crisp autumn breeze rustled through what was left of the leaves on the giant oak trees around the house of Oakhurst. Shea locked the door behind her and stepped out into the bright morning sunshine. She never tired of her walk to work and counted herself most fortunate to have landed in such a magnificent spot.

Faeries, Sprites and Lights was only a few months ago, but it seemed like forever. Though the time flew by, Oakhurst seemed as though it had always been her home. She was its protector now, its Guardian, and she took that honor quite seriously.

Her role had become somewhat tricky following the ruckus in the garden and the subsequent demise of Darius Pendragon at the hands of the dragon. It was one thing to try to explain the whole thing to the humans, but an entirely different one to convince them that she needed to remain in possession of the relics of the Dragon Triad.

Upon her return from London, Lucy Abernathy was most taken in by Shea's tales of what had happened in the gardens. She was surprised and, as Shea expected, quite disappointed in Pendragon's duplicitous agenda. Out of all of the humans she dealt with, it was Lucy who took the most convincing.

"Shea, you don't seem to understand," Lucy told her. "I cannot simply 'give' you the relics. There are protocols in these matters. There are international agreements between museums – between *governments* – that must be considered. To just let you have them could lead to an international incident."

Shea sighed. "I understand that," she answered, "but if something is not done to secure them, there may be an incident between kingdoms in the garden that could spill over from the fae realm into the human realm." The expression on Lucy's face told Shea she wasn't completely buying it. "Look, I know this is all unbelievable, but this is important."

"Shea, I –"

"I would not have asked were it not so."

Dismay crossed Lucy's face. Shea could tell her friend knew the task she asked would be difficult, and she held her breath.

After a long moment, Lucy nodded.

"Let me see what I can do."

🙰 ☙

The amulet still hung from Shea's neck. That one was the easiest to keep in her possession for the simple fact it had been there since the time of her arrival in the human realm. They allowed her to keep the staff as well, and she was often spotted in the gardens using it as what most folks simply assumed was nothing more than a rather large, fancy walking stick. But the Keeper of Time was another matter.

In discussions with Evangeline Monteague, President of Minnetrista, Lucy, and several other upper-level members of the staff, it was agreed upon that the Keeper of Time would be stored securely in Collections. Lucy had somehow managed to convince the British Museum to continue to loan it to them indefinitely, but she knew that wouldn't last forever. Shea was satisfied with the fact that it would give her enough time to seek further counsel from Queen Liliana on how best to proceed.

Oh, how she missed Elisabeth! For one who appeared so young, she carried such wisdom and knowledge. And, of course, her surprising transformation just prior to her exit from the gardens revealed that she was so much more than her nine year-old countenance portrayed her to be. What she wouldn't give for her counsel on these matters now!

Some days Shea just wished it could all go away – all the responsibilities, all the protocol, all the duties associated with being Guardian to the kingdoms in and around Oakhurst.

All of it, that is, except for Connor and what they had

60

together in the realm of humans.

ဆ   ﾒﾒ

Queen Liliana sat upon her throne pondering her options. She wanted to take counsel with Verena but knew that her daughter was more distracted these days, to the point where it was nearly useless talking to her at all. On the occasions when they would converse, Verena would look at her pretending to listen, but a mother's instinct knows when a daughter is tuning her out. And these days, Verena was definitely tuning her mother out.

Though she had made herself quite clear to Shea, Guardian of Oakhurst, the queen had her doubts about whether or not the girl would actually carry out her assigned task. She was almost obedient to a fault, and Liliana had made an attempt to use that to her own full advantage. However, her intel indicated otherwise.

Her son was another matter altogether. Liliana knew that Connor had fallen for Shea from the first moment he had come to her in human form. And recently, the prince had made no efforts to hide his preoccupation with the girl nor his new-found predilection for rooting around in the dirt.

The winter solstice would be upon them in a short time, and if Shea were unable to complete her mission, the queen knew she would have to take matters into her own hands. Perhaps sooner rather than later, for the simple fact that if Shea did not see it coming, she would have no way of defending against it.

And Queen Liliana was counting on that.

CHAPTER 8

Shea lay on the sleeping porch on the second floor of
Oakhurst wrapped and toasty like a baked potato in a thick,
down comforter. It had been an exhausting Saturday afternoon
and evening with three weddings taking place on the grounds
over the weekend. Autumn was always a popular time with the
change in foliage, and though the weather was often
unpredictable, if luck was on the bride's side, the wedding and
subsequent photographs were always stunning. Minnetrista
definitely knew how to do weddings up right.

Her hair had grown back out in the months following the
attack of the celestial faeries. Now that she had regained her
memory, Shea no longer dreaded going to sleep and no longer
feared the return of the wicked fae. She now welcomed the
dreams, and it was almost as if she were able to return home.
She relished the nights where her father and brothers would

63

come to her in dreams sharing news of their latest victories or offering sage advice.

On occasion Arn would be there, too, with his ready smile and steadfast loyalty. He was the truest friend she had ever known – as close as family, and she missed him as much as any of the others. She loved waking from a dream of Arn, mostly because she was able to carry it with her throughout the day, and it always brought a smile to her face.

Shea drifted off relatively quickly on this night and fell into a dream almost immediately. It was dark, but by the light of the full moon she could see the silhouette of Castle Ravensforge as it had once been. She took flight, a sensation she had never before experienced in a dream.

She passed high above the walls and towers of the palace soaring ever skyward as she circled the estate before flying off to the north. Over the forest and meadows she went, feeling the freedom of the wind in her face as she flew onward. To her right, a raven flew alongside her. He was much bigger than she, but she felt him more a kindred spirit than a threat.

She knew where they were going, even though she had only been there once when she was very young. She was somewhat trepidatious, yet eager to see her destination: the fabled forges of Ravensforge.

Shea lit upon a rock just outside the cavernous entrance to the Forge. Her father had spoken of it many times throughout her childhood, and it held a special place in her heart. This was where her story began. This is where the tradition of the Guard had formed, straight from the fires of Ravensforge. It was here that all Guard in the fae realm originated. Guntram and his sons and daughter, and even Arland of Oakhurst, their tradition was born out of the flames here.

The same was true of their weaponry. It was a source of pride for the rulers of Ravensforge. None finer in all the realm, and they alone possessed them. They alone were responsible for determining who would carry them. And they were the sole source of the Swords of Nobility.

Shea entered slowly and immediately felt the warmth from within on her face. The fires burned brightly in the chamber ahead, and she walked to the mouth of the room. It was empty, save for the flames that burned in the center of the room. The craftsmen were all gone. She walked to the forge and looked closely into the flames. Without warning, the flames died instantly leaving only a pit of glowing embers.

"You look perplexed, Shea of Ravensforge," came a raspy voice from behind her. She did not recognize it and wheeled about to find herself face-to-face with a troll. She had smelled him before she saw him and was somewhat startled at his appearance. He wore a furry vest that was matted and dirty with boots that reached nearly to his knees. His legs were covered with brown breeches, and he looked as though he'd crawled into the cavern. But the most startling thing about his appearance was his face: he had only one good eye. The other was covered by an eye patch, and his hair was a wild, unkempt gray.

"Where has everyone gone?" she asked the troll, not sure she wanted the answer.

"They have escaped," the troll answered matter-of-factly, "to parts unknown."

"Why?" Shea asked. "Why have they left their post?"

"The Dark Warrior approached, ready to take this stronghold, so those who were here hid the Forge by way of magic so he would not be able to use it for his evil purpose."

65

"Which is what?"

"Unknown," the troll replied. "But it was just another piece to the puzzle, one more element to the power he craves. Once he possesses all the elements, both relics and strongholds, nothing can stop him, both in this realm and the next."

"The human realm?"

"Yes."

Shea looked around her. There were only a handful of swords hanging in the racks on the walls. "Who commissioned these?"

"Beltran, before the fall of Ravensforge."

"Who will they go to now?"

"The one who holds the key to the kingdom," the troll answered gravely. "He who would be king will most assuredly take his place as such one day. But until then, he must –"

Shea caught her breath. Her eyes were bleary in the early morning light, and she found herself back on the sleeping porch at Oakhurst. Though she tried to fall back asleep, her mind kept turning the troll's words over in her head again and again to no avail.

For now, the dream would have to remain a misty riddle to be solved later.

        ☙   ❧

The cold November rain beat down on the windows of Oakhurst as Shea hauled boxes one by one from the second floor storage closet to the basement. They were light in weight but somewhat awkward and unwieldy, and she took care not to drop them as they were filled with antique glass Christmas ornaments from Elisabeth's collection.

The decorations ladies had set up shop in the main room of the basement that was two over from the laundry and merrily went about planning the decorations for the Enchanted Luminaria, which was scheduled for the first weekend in December.

It was an informal event, one that was enjoyed by families in the surrounding community and was a beautiful way to show them what Oakhurst looked like when Elisabeth and her family lived there in the early 1900s. It was a different era to be sure, but one well worth remembering nonetheless.

"Some traditions are dying out," GiGi had said in the last committee meeting, and that sentiment had resonated most among the more seasoned volunteers. They sat around the table laughing as they talked about how it had been growing up in the nineteen-sixties.

"Why, I remember it just wasn't proper for a young man to honk his horn if he was there to pick you up for a date."

"How true!" said another. "My father made sure they came up to the door to meet *him*."

"My granddaughter's dates *text* her when they are out in the driveway!" said a third. This comment brought gasps and nods all around the table.

"My father had a brass '*ahh*-oooooo-*gaaah*' horn," said the fourth of the ladies with a rather sheepish grin on her face.

"A what?" asked the first woman.

"Oh, you know, said the fourth, making her hand like it was squeezing the rubber bulb of an old-fashioned brass car horn. *"Ahh*-ooooo-*gaaah!"*

"Aahhh," the ladies all nodded in understanding.

"He would lie in wait until we would return from our date," she said, leaning over the table as if to impart some deep, dark, secret. "Then, just when my feller would lean in to kiss me...*Ahh*-ooooo-*gaaah!*"

The women all cackled with glee returning to their Christmas decorations. Shea shook her head with a smile as she stacked the boxes next to the table.

It would prove to be an interesting season indeed.

ℬ   ℭ

The humans had just celebrated what they called "Thanksgiving" a few days before. Sam had invited Shea and Connor to his home to share in the festivities with his family, and it had been a wonderful day. Extended family, lots of new and wonderful foods, and a most peculiar ritual of sitting around after the meal watching grown men dressed in the strangest battle armor Shea had ever seen fight over an odd-shaped ball.

"Football," Sam had called it, looking perplexed that Shea nor Connor neither one had ever heard of it. Nonetheless, it had been a wonderful day.

Overnight, Thanksgiving transformed into the human holiday called "Christmas," celebrated over a month's time with shopping and baking and decorating and gifts and more sweets than anyone should ever even think about consuming. Somewhat befuddled, Shea simply went along with the flow. One thing was certain: Oakhurst looked beautiful decorated for Christmas, and she counted herself lucky to be there.

As if by magic, the Minnetrista campus was transformed into a Christmas wonderland. White twinkle lights hung

68

everywhere adding a sense of magic, and tasteful decorations of garlands, tinsel, and ornaments lent a feel of home to the place. Shea liked to imagine what Oakhurst must have been like with Elisabeth and her family living up and down the boulevard.

The houses of Oakhurst and Nebosham were dressed in their holiday finery. Nebosham had a variety of Christmas trees throughout the house and decorated to the nines, each with an individual theme. Oakhurst was adorned with Christmas décor with a faerie twist. Winter-themed miniature homes, shops, and an ice palace were crafted by a group of local artists, making the house an exciting place to tour.

Shea loved the house and was happy to see it being used in such a way. She had a great appreciation for the humans who knew the treasure that Oakhurst and the gardens truly were and was sure that Elisabeth would approve. Adjusting to the human realm was going better than she'd anticipated, both for her and Connor. Her longing for Ravensforge fading, Shea began to consider making this her home forever.

But there was sadness creeping into Shea's happy home, for she knew that the winter solstice would soon be upon them and that time was growing short for her and Connor.

Shea decided, even if it meant facing the queen's wrath, she would enjoy every moment she had left with him. And that would have to be enough.

CHAPTER 9

The snow fell softly on the grounds of Oakhurst. Connor finished lighting the last of his assigned luminaria that lined the pathways throughout the gardens. Snowflakes caught on his lashes, and he brushed them away from his line of vision as he watched the main gate. The guests for the Enchanted Luminaria were beginning to arrive, and he smiled at the thought of what awaited them for the evening.

It had been five months since the incident in the Gardens at Faeries, Sprites, and Lights. And though Muncie, Indiana, would never forget the dragon or the young woman who tamed it, memories were short, and there were stories to be told yet again.

Shea had regained nearly all her memories of her life at Ravensforge, and though they both knew it to be truthful and real, the good folk of Muncie saw the whole dragon incident as little more than great storytelling and casual entertainment. Best of all, according to Sam Cooke, it was a way to draw guests through the gates, and that, he concluded, was always a plus.

Connor headed up to the house from the main gate. The cold December air chilled him, mostly because he wasn't particularly dressed for it. Darla Stevens, from the Theatrical and Outreach Department, had set him up with a "princely" costume, which really wasn't much different than what he wore on state occasions for the Kingdom of Oakhurst. But that seemed like so long ago.

A figure down Aunt Emma's path caught his eye, and Connor paused, watching as it came through the service gate. The figure's walk was familiar to him, but he couldn't make out a face in the twilight. Since he was running a little behind, he waved and headed up to the back door of Oakhurst.

He stomped the snow from his boots and opened the door, stepping in from the cold.

"Oh, good, you're here," Alexandra called to him from the foyer. "Have you seen Shea?"

Connor brushed the snow from his hair, stomping his feet for good measure on the doormat. "No, not yet. Why?"

"Just curious. She hasn't come down yet." She moved toward him, leaning in and whispering, "Is she okay with her costume?"

Just then Shea came down to the landing from her tiny second floor apartment. What Connor saw made him catch his breath, and he felt his face flush as he looked up at her.

Shea stood on the landing. Most of what she wore he had seen before, but it was the finishing touches that GiGi had added that made all the difference. She was dressed in her battle armor, and the ruby eye of the raven on her breastplate glistened. She had on a pair of breeches and boots that nearly came to the bottom of her knees. They were made of doeskin and fit close to her calves. But the most spectacular piece of her attire for the evening was a beautiful snow leopard cape that fell at the back of her knees. A hood hung down off her shoulders and made her look as if she'd just stepped out of a faerie tale.

"What?" Shea asked him, suddenly feeling self-conscious. "Does it look that bad?"

Alexandra found the words when Connor had none. "Wow. You look stunning."

"Is that good?" Shea asked, unsure of the context. Usually, in her world, stunning someone was not a good thing.

Alexandra laughed. "Yes," she answered, looking to Connor who still stood dumbstruck. "Yes, it's *very* good." She chuckled at the naiveté of her friends, shook her head and walked away, leaving the pair in the back stairwell.

Shea descended the stairs and met Connor at the door. She reached up, brushing the remaining snow from his shoulders. He leaned in and kissed her, and she placed her hand on his cheek. It was cold to the touch, and she stepped back and smiled at him. "So I don't look ridiculous?"

"No," Connor replied, with a knowing smile. "Not at all. I'd say GiGi did a fine job. Is this not like what you wore at home?"

"Close," she answered, "although the fur is a bit much. We only used it for trim."

"Well, we just won't tell anyone," Connor said, with a wink.

Shea reached up and punched him playfully in the

shoulder. "Is Verena coming this evening?"

"She said she was, but who knows these days?"

The loss of Royce had been harder on her than most around her realized, but she confided in Connor and Shea often in terms of how she was feeling. The incident had shaken her deeply, and she was distant most days. Queen Liliana worried and continued to press Connor for details. Not one to break a trust, Connor would only do his best to reassure his mother as she still struggled with his inability to return home. Though he was hopeful that he might be able to resolve the situation one day, he knew that time was not on his side.

Because time passes differently in the human realm than in the fae realm, he had already noticed changes in himself that he knew were not good. While those in the kingdom still looked as he remembered them from before his arrival here, he felt himself begin to change in ways he couldn't describe. This made him uneasy, if only because the permanence of his situation was beginning to sink in.

And yet, how could he argue with being forever "trapped" in the human realm with Shea. His feelings for her grew stronger by the day, and he so enjoyed spending time with her. It was mundane tasks that he relished most. Going to the grocery, sharing a meal together, sitting with her at one of any number of special events at Minnetrista. Sometimes Sam Cooke would give them tickets to the symphony or the theatre, and they would go out like a nice, normal *human* couple.

But it was the look in his mother's eyes when he met with her regularly that told him he could never stay.

And then there was the matter of the Princesses of Ravensforge. They might very well be the last remaining citizens of Ravensforge, save for Minister Foley who had mysteriously and conveniently disappeared once his duplicitous actions had been discovered. Connor had vowed that he would pay for what he had done should the Prince of Oakhurst ever catch up with him in either realm.

Connor reached out and took Shea's hand and led her through the dining room. "Which story are you sharing with the guests this evening?"

Shea shrugged. "I'm not sure yet. I'm still trying to get a handle on this whole Christmas thing. Probably the closest thing we had at Ravensforge was the king's Winter Ball. It was the most beautiful event you've ever seen."

"I've seen some pretty amazing things in the Great Hall of Ravensforge." He meant her, but knew she would think of the state dinner and his betrothal.

"Yes, but this was something even beyond that. When winter is upon us, the swordsmiths return to the palace with the newest weapons for the king's inspection and blessing. If they pass muster, they are presented to the next round of recruits for the Guard."

Shea paused a moment as she realized that the Winter Ball would never happen again.

Connor gave her a weak, yet knowing smile. "I'm sorry," was all he could bring himself to say. She smiled at him in return and squeezed his hand, glad to have him by her side.

"Oh, good, I'm glad I found you!" came a delighted squeal from across the room. It was GiGi, and she was in a hurry as usual. She hustled across the room grabbing Shea's hands up in her own. "Your costume looks *fabulous*, by the way! The new costumer has outdone herself this time!"

GiGi's enthusiasm was met with blank stares from both of them. "Well!" she said, clapping her hands together for emphasis. "Time to get this show on the road! Are you ready?"

Shea sighed and headed across the foyer and into the library. The whole house was beautifully decorated for the season with lush reds and greens accentuating every room for the holiday. White lights covered two matching trees that mirrored one another in the center of the room bringing a crisp, new sense of style to the old house. Although this was Shea's first Christmas, she knew it was a magical season for the humans, full of a sense of wonder and warmth and love.

Shea decided it was something she could adapt to gladly.

ও   ೞ

The snow continued to fall as guests huddled in around Shea on the front porch of Oakhurst. It was spacious, almost like a room outside, with enough space for at least a dozen guests to huddle around as they listened to her tale. It was lit with a beautiful fixture overhead, and the lights from inside the house cast a sense of magic onto the space. Shea stood beneath the porch light, the fur cape draped softly over her shoulders and Dragon Staff in hand, looking as if she'd stepped straight out of a faerie tale.

Her role was to set the mood for the visitors so that they might experience some sense of magic while there.

"Good evening," she greeted the guests with a smile, "and welcome to Oakhurst. I am Shea, Guardian of Oakhurst and protector of those fae and sprites who make their home here in the gardens."

"Queen Liliana of Oakhurst and King Rogan of Nebosham bid you welcome as well. They are always glad to have human guests among us."

"I came from the Kingdom of Ravensforge in the faerie realm. There we celebrated the coming of winter with a special ball. King Beltran would call upon the Master Swordsmith and his craftsmen from the Forge, and they would bring down the swords they had crafted over the past season. The king would bless each of the swords and hand them over to the newest members of the Guard."

A sad smile crossed her face as she thought of her family.

"There is a celebration like none you have ever seen filled with family and friends, music and dance. And lights everywhere! Very much like this place. Truly, it is a magical time."

She went on to share more of the celebration when a little boy no more than four years old spoke up. "Does Santa Claus come, too?" he asked.

Shea had heard of Santa Claus but knew very little of him. GiGi had told her to tread lightly where this subject was concerned because not every family handled Christmas in the same way. *"Middle of the road is best,"* GiGi told her.

"I have never met Santa Claus at one of King Beltran's celebrations," Shea answered honestly.

"What about baby Jesus?" a little girl piped in. She appeared to be little more than six years old, and she and her little sister were both bundled in matching pink coats and fluffy white scarves. "He's a king, too. Maybe he knows your king."

Shea knelt before the little girl. "A baby who is a king?" she asked. This was a foreign concept to her.

The little girl smiled and nodded.

"Perhaps later you could tell me more?" Shea asked the

little girl. The child looked up at her mother who nodded, then turned back to Shea and nodded emphatically.

The little girl looked up at her in earnest. "Three kings came to worship him. They followed a star to find him."

"In his palace?" Shea asked.

"No, silly," the little girl replied. "Baby Jesus was born in a manger."

"A manger? What is that?"

"It's a thing that horses eat out of, in a barn," the little one said matter-of-factly. "There was another king who didn't like him very much. He wanted to hurt the baby Jesus."

"Well, this king of yours, does he have a Guardian? Someone who will defend his life? Keep him safe?" Shea asked, trying to put it in a context she might understand.

"Oh, no, he doesn't need anyone to keep him safe." The girl paused, drawing in near to Shea. "But if you ask him to, he will keep you safe."

The girl's little sister, no more than three, smiled shyly and asked Shea, "Are you a princess?"

Shea smiled. "No. No, I'm not."

"Well, you should be."

Shea's stomach turned at the child's comment. The winter solstice was barely two weeks away, and time was running out for her and Connor and what they had together. It was for his own good and for the good of the kingdom she told herself, as she tried to justify her duplicitousness. She knew in the end it would not be pleasant for anyone, least of all, her. She just hoped that after it was all over that Connor would understand why she had gone along with his mother's plan.

"Thank you," she told the little girl, placing her hand upon the child's head. "That means a lot."

CHAPTER 10

The first night of Minnetrista's Enchanted Luminaria in the can, Shea set about closing down the house for the night. She helped the volunteers clean up after the guests, then locked up the house before heading upstairs. She was looking forward to getting out of her get-up and settling in for the night.

It was then she realized she hadn't seen Connor since the guests had left. It wasn't like him to just disappear without saying goodbye. Perhaps GiGi had sent him on a last minute mission back up to the Center. Shea decided to change clothes and wait around for him just in case.

Shutting off the lights on the main floor, first in the library, then the foyer and dining room, she headed for the back stairs when something caught her eye. A soft glow came from the upstairs window in the door that led to the sleeping porch. She thought she had cleared everyone out but gave that notion a second thought as she moved slowly up the stairs.

Instinctively her hand moved toward the sword on her hip as she edged silently toward the door. She hadn't seen anything out of the ordinary since the Gutiku had departed the gardens back in July, but she didn't want to take any chances. Looking through the window as she reached the landing, Shea could hardly believe her eyes and relaxed as she opened the door.

The sleeping porch was lit with close to a hundred candles placed all about. The flames flickered as the breeze came in through the screens and the vents on the floor. Though it was cold outside, the porch was cozy. Outside, all was calm as the snow fell silently on the gardens of Oakhurst.

Shea caught her breath. It was even more beautiful than the winter celebration had ever been at Ravensforge! She wandered over to the wicker sofa. On the small table in the center of the room was a modest offering of bread, cheese, and meats.

"I know it's not exactly like home," Connor said from the opposite corner of the porch, "but it's as close as I could find."

Shea smiled as she looked around. "It's wonderful," she said, as he came to her. "Thank you."

She looked up at him as he took her face in his hands and leaned in to kiss her. Her mind nagged at her to pull away, that surely the queen was having them watched, but found she could not. The warmth of his kiss took the edge off of the cold night air through the screens, and Shea wished to stay in that moment forever.

They sat down and shared the meal together, laughing and reminiscing about home and the things they missed the most.

"If you could go home for one day and do anything – anything at all – what would you do?" Connor asked her finally.

Shea thought for a moment, her eyes wistful as she looked out over the snow-covered garden. "See my family…any of them. Even if it were just one of them, that would be my wish."

She could tell immediately that Connor wished he hadn't asked. She could see her own sadness reflected back in his eyes.

She was beautiful in the candlelight, hauntingly so, and though she thought she looked ridiculous in the fur cape, he thought her to be the most incredible thing he'd ever seen.

"You're lucky, you know," she told Connor. "You still have your family. You can see them, talk to them, anytime you want."

"I wish we could both go home," Connor said. "Then you could become part of my family. They would love you." He stopped himself, fearing he'd already said too much.

Shea blushed in the candlelight. "I hardly think your mother is very fond of me," she said, raising her eyebrows.

"She only knows you as Guardian to Oakhurst. And Nebosham. She understands all that your station entails. Surely she would see you differently in our realm." *Empty, hollow words*, he added silently, knowing that would never be possible.

"Do you think we will ever find a way to get both of us back home?"

Connor sighed, as he thought back to the magical potion that failed to return him to the fae realm. His mother was disappointed, but secretly Connor was relieved.

"Maybe if they find another portal," he said finally.

"Yes, but can you go back through the portal if we are to locate one?" Shea asked, hoping for a different answer this time.

He shook his head. "The remnants of the dark magic within me would prove most…unpleasant."

Shea smiled at him. "Then this will be enough," she said. She leaned in and kissed him.

For now, it would have to be.

CHAPTER 11

The snow glistened in the sunlight as Shea stepped out into the beautiful Saturday morning. Though it was the weekend, it was another day of work at Oakhurst for the simple fact that it was the second day of the Enchanted Luminaria. The night before had been magical, and she was excited about the second night but knew there was also half a day's work ahead.

The sidewalks had been cleared by the grounds crew already, and she headed up toward the boulevard when something in the front yard caught her eye. She took care not to mar the fresh snow on the lawn and went up the front walk.

What appeared to be a traveling cloak was caught on the bushes to the left of the front porch. It was covered with some snow but not frozen stiff yet. Unsure if it belonged to one of the actors placed around the gardens the night before or one of the guests, Shea picked it up, brushed it off, and laid it gently over the edge of the front porch. Her hope was that whomever had misplaced it would come looking for it.

From her vantage point on the top step of the porch, she noticed footprints going around the side of the house. She thought that odd and followed them. What she discovered unnerved her somewhat.

The tracks went around the house, stopping at each window as if whomever it was they belonged to had been peering inside. Some of the windows were high and would have been difficult to see in, but others gave them a clear view of what was going on inside. Not your usual way to check out the house, but then again maybe it was someone who had missed the festivities and gotten there a bit too late.

Filing it away in her mind for later, she would have to remember to say something to security about it.

Coming around the back side of the house, Shea stomped the snow off her boots, pulled her collar up and headed up toward the Center. It was going to be a glorious day, and she was happy to be at Oakhurst.

ප   ශ

In the blue light of early evening a gentle snow began to fall again on what was already three inches on the ground from the night before. The grounds crew had done a good job of keeping it cleared away for the Luminaria event, but it looked as if the snow was going to have the last word on the issue on this night.

Shea had been on the front porch of Oakhurst all evening, greeting guests and telling tales from the faerie realm. There was a sharp breeze blowing through the porch and for once, Shea was glad to have on the heavy fur cape. She put the hood up for awhile and managed to stay quite toasty most of the evening.

She saw Verena on the other side of the porch and waved. Verena acknowledged her before tagging along with a group of human visitors as they headed into the house through the front door. Shea was just glad to see her and hoped she would spend some time with Connor before heading back to their mother's palace.

⁎ ⁍

In the upstairs gallery just across the hall from Shea's tiny apartment sat a fantastic display of faerie relics, most of which had been on display at Faeries, Sprites, and Lights a few months before. Because they were on loan, Lucy wanted to take full advantage of them before having to ship the bulk of them back to the British Museum in early January.

They had been quite a coup in spite of the circumstances surrounding their arrival and the subsequent demise of one Darius Pendragon. An unsavory character at best, the humans weren't quite sure what to make of him, but Shea and a handful of fae knew him for exactly who and what he was: Messenger to the Dark Warrior of Erebos.

Unseen by human eyes as the guests filed through the gallery, a dozen fae warriors stood guard hovering around the Keeper of Time. Not to be outdone by Liliana's forces, King Rogan sent twenty sprites to guard the doors to the gallery.

The relic was magnificent under the gallery lights. The patinaed bronze dragon jealously guarded the egg, and its fiery

85

eyes glowed just as they had in the garden a few months before. It almost looked content to be guarded.

Though small in size, all who stood watch were fierce in countenance and true to their post, pledging none would reach the prize in their keep.

ঙ০   ৪৩

The crowd swirled around Shea and Connor on the main floor of Oakhurst, oftentimes taking up the space between them as well. Guests made their way through the house which had been decorated to the hilt for the Christmas holiday. Rooms were filled with Christmas trees, garlands and lights, and the dining room was set for a formal family dinner. Other staff members shared stories of Elisabeth Ball and her family and how they had celebrated the holidays in the early 1900s. While it had been a most enjoyable evening, Shea had to admit she was tired. It was the end of the second night, and though she loved to tell stories, she was flat out exhausted.

Shea continued to say hello to the children who asked all sorts of questions: "Are you a faerie princess?" or "Are you one of Santa's elves?" or just "You sure are pretty." She was not used to this type of attention, and while she enjoyed sharing the lore of Oakhurst and Ravensforge with the humans, she began to realize that they didn't really understand that most of what she was saying was true.

One of the guests brushed past Shea, and the smell coming off of him nearly made her gag. He was dressed for the weather in a bushy fur vest, and his head was covered by a black hood of a traveling cloak similar to the one she had found that morning in the front yard. Shea was beginning to think she had missed something in the staff meeting where they discussed characters, but she was certain GiGi would never encourage staff to show up smelling quite that foul. Lending authenticity to your story was one thing, but this was taking it just a little too far.

Her eyes followed him as he joined a crowd of people headed up to the second floor galleries. Shea reminded herself she would need to watch for him and make sure he didn't cause any trouble. Something with him just didn't sit right, and she couldn't shake the feeling that there was more to the smelly visitor than met the eye.

One thing her father had taught her: expect trouble and you won't be surprised when it shows up.

೧೦   ೦೮

"Mommy, *look!* It's the dragon we saw this summer in the garden!" squealed a little boy in delight as he ran up to the pedestal where the Keeper of Time rested. Its fiery eyes shone brilliantly as it gazed back at the lad under the gallery lights, making it a spectacular display at his eye level.

"Yes, honey, it's the dragon," his mother replied. The look in her eyes told all she couldn't – that she still hadn't quite processed the whole drama that had unfolded before them.

A handful of guests straggled through the upstairs gallery. It was nearly nine o'clock, and the crowd had thinned to a trickle over the past half hour. The relic sat in its place of honor in the center of the room under gallery lighting, and the dragon's eyes glowed as if flames burned within them.

The few who remained in the gallery sniffed at the air as they began to notice a rather putrid odor. Looking around they saw the smelly stranger as he entered the room, and they gathered their children and made a hasty exit.

The stranger stood alone in the gallery, at least to human eyes, but the fae and sprite guards sprung into action. Swords and arrows and daggers flew in the intruder's direction in a bold attempt to stop him or at least impede his progress, but to no avail. Swatting at them like so many bugs in the woods, the intruder easily cleared his way to the prize he had come for.

CHAPTER 12

From the gallery at the far end of the house, Verena could hear the warriors of Oakhurst causing such a commotion it was a wonder the humans *didn't* hear them! Shouts of *"Stop!"* and *"Get him!"* rang out, filling the second floor of the house with a racket such as it had probably never heard.

Exchanging glances with Rayne, Verena took flight from atop the mantel and glided along the ceiling toward the far gallery. Her heart raced, uncertain of what she would find. She knew that her mother had sent guards to stand watch over the Keeper of Time but was floored by the melee that greeted her when she cleared the second doorway.

In the center of the gallery, standing hunched over the Keeper, was a human – of sorts. He was dressed in a traveling cloak and something made of fur, but he wore a hood and his face was obscured from her vantage point. Swarming around his head were the warriors from Oakhurst Palace. They hammered at him, but he batted them away like nothing. At his feet the sprites stabbed at his boots and made attempts to climb up his legs, but it seemed to make little difference.

Shocked at the sight, Rayne began to protest. "Princess, I do not think it wise –"

Without a word, Verena headed toward the ruckus. She flew in closer and immediately knew that the intruder was not human at all but instead a creature that had come from the faerie realm. He was not tall, more the size of a young human teenager. She had to dodge flying weapons and an occasional warrior as she made a swift approach.

The creature reached down and pulled a velveteen pouch from his belt. Unabashedly, he snatched the Keeper from its perch and stuffed it into the bag, pulling the drawstring tight around the top of it.

Seeing her chance, Verena swooped in and grabbed hold of the cord on the bag and tried to at least yank it out of the intruder's hands so that King Rogan's men could hide it away. Misjudging the stranger's strength, she reached the end of the cord and stopped dead making a backward-sprawling flight straight into the being's chest.

Holding on for dear life, she clung to the cord and dangled below the bag. The intruder lifted the bag up so that he could closer inspect the one who had made a feeble attempt to steal his prize.

A sudden charge by Rayne didn't even faze the intruder. Sword drawn, the guard rushed at him, ready to cut the cord Verena hung by. She was startled by the creature's reflexes and was swiftly swatted to the floor.

What Verena saw next nearly took her breath away as she looked upon the creature's face. She gasped as he backhanded her, sending the princess flying across the gallery. She smacked hard into the wall and fell to the floor unconscious.

Without so much as a second glance, the intruder made a hasty retreat and headed back down the front stairs of Oakhurst.

   ❧   ❧

Shea made her way across the foyer to the dining room where Connor stood talking with a small group of guests. When he had finished, she approached.

"Did you see that guy that went through here a minute ago?"

"Uh, which one? There have been lots of guys through here this evening," Connor teased her, and he was right.

"You'd have remembered this one," she replied. "He looked a little on the scruffy side and smelled as though he'd been living in the garbage dumpster for quite some time."

"Really?"

"Yeah, it was pretty bad."

"Not the usual crowd, huh?" Connor asked.

"Not exactly," Shea agreed. "Maybe he was just trying to get in out of the cold."

Connor sighed as he glanced around. "About time to wrap it up, isn't it? I don't know about you, but I'm beat."

It had been a long day, and they still had a ways to go before either of them could rest, but the end was in sight. Shea walked back over to the library and waited until the last of the evening's guests filtered through the secret entrance to the screened-in porch, then made sure they'd exited into the back garden before locking the door behind them.

She closed the secret passageway and traced her steps back through the library, winding her way through what was left of the crowd and nodding to folks who greeted her as she went. The Dragon Staff was a good foot taller than she was, and people took notice of the headpiece as it began to glow. The hood of Shea's fur cape rested upon her shoulders giving her a regal sort of look as she crossed the room. The amulet around her neck resonated as it rested just beneath the raven on her breastplate, the bird's ruby eye glistening as it reflected back the Christmas lights.

Shea reached the door of library and quickly scanned the foyer for Connor who was nowhere to be found. As the people began to move out, she stood in the doorway behind the handful of guests who were taking their time and enjoying the view.

It was then that she saw him.

The furry guy walked back through the dining room and waited until the last of the guests filtered through toward the back door, then made his way toward the front door like a salmon swimming upstream. He reeked and from her vantage point in the door of the library, Shea smelled him before she saw him. She looked across the foyer, and her eyes locked with Connor's. The smelly stranger was between them, hood still up, head down, and moving quickly toward the door.

And he had something in his hands.

ᗡ   ᘓ

Connor saw Shea pointing but he already knew who the intruder was by the stench. He would never forget that smell or the night that brought him to this place. Connor tried to get

92

through the crowd, but a family with four children stood between him and the door. He waited until they filed by, then practically ran to the door as the stranger took the door knob in hand.

Connor reached up and grabbed the stranger by the shoulder wheeling him about. What stood facing him was utterly shocking.

It was the one-eyed troll – *the same one who had sent him to Oakhurst a few months prior!* The same troll to whom he had bargained away the Sword of Nobility. The same horrid, smelly troll except for one thing: the one good eye he did have was now black as night and offered up no reflection nor indicated that there was any soul behind it whatsoever.

The soulless black eye stared back at him, not even acknowledging that he knew who Connor was. The troll snarled at him, and just as Connor noticed the velveteen bag in his hand – *the same one that had previously held the Keeper of Time* – the troll swung it upward, soundly clocking Connor on the side of his head. Half a second later the Prince of Oakhurst lay in a crumpled heap in the doorway of the house.

Shocked by the assault, Shea rushed to Connor's side as the nasty troll made his escape down the steps and across the yard. Finding Connor unconscious, she tried to rouse him. When he began to stir, she pulled him up and leaned him against the doorway.

"The Keeper," Connor said breathlessly. "He took the Keeper."

Dragon Staff in hand, Shea bounded off the porch of Oakhurst and sprinted to the gate. Across the boulevard she could just make out the furry, smelly figure as it disappeared into the darkness bound by the tree line at the top of the ridge.

She half-ran, half-slid across the narrow boulevard, then braked with her free hand as she caught hold of a sapling at the edge of the ridge. She stopped just long enough to look down the steep slope that ended some thirty feet below in the White River.

She could see him hurtling down the hillside at a breakneck pace, and she knew she had to stop him. If he truly had the Keeper of Time in his possession, Rogan would have no reason to hold back from waging war on Oakhurst, and it would be on her head.

The snow fell harder as Shea made her way down the hill, getting her feet tangled only once in the dry, dead weeds hidden beneath the snow. She used the staff several times to help steady herself as she managed a rapid descent toward the frozen river below. The snowflakes were sticking to her lashes, and it was getting harder to see what waited for her below.

Shea reached the river's edge and stopped suddenly. There, standing in the middle of the river, was the troll holding the Keeper of Time in one hand as he dropped the velveteen bag on the ice. A glance back up the hill told her Connor had righted himself and was not far behind. She could hear him shouting to her but couldn't make out what he was saying.

Looking back at the troll, she stepped out on the ice.

        ಐ   ಛ

From the hilltop Connor could barely see Shea and the troll through the falling snow. The troll's magic was tied to the water, and Connor did not see this ending well. She looked up at him from the water's edge.

"Shea, stay off the ice!" he called to her. He watched as she stepped out onto the frozen river, moving until she was a short distance from the troll.

"No," Connor groaned, as he started down the slope.

ᔰ   ᔱ

"You have something that doesn't belong to you, troll," Shea warned, as she stepped toward him, closing the distance between them. The staff head began to glow as she rested the end of it on the ice next to her. The amulet hidden beneath her breastplate began to resonate as it usually did when the three relics were in such close proximity. But this time it felt different. "Return it, and no harm will come to you."

The troll raised the Keeper as the dragon's eyes began to glow casting an eerie light upon his dreadful face and his lone, black eye. "You have some things that don't belong to *you*, Shea of Ravensforge," the troll growled, "and I have been sent to take them back."

Shea's arm holding the staff became suddenly aware of the weight of it. The staff felt as if it weighed twice what it had only moments before! She shifted it slightly giving her arm a little respite.

"I think not," Shea replied, as she moved the staff from her right hand to her left. Though that arm was just as strong as the other, it almost felt as if the staff's weight had increased again in the moment she'd been standing there. She brought the tip of it down on the ice and heard a sharp *CRACK!*

Shea looked around trying to judge the distance from the shore. Though it wasn't far, she wasn't sure she could make it to the riverbank dragging the staff along with her but leaving it

95

to the troll was not an option. She reached for her sword with her right hand, but the staff nearly knocked her off balance, and it was all she could do to right it with both hands.

The ice beneath her creaked and groaned as Shea wrapped both arms around the staff.

"Oh," snarled the troll, *"I think so."*

"Shea!" Connor shouted, as he barreled headlong down the slope. The riverbank came up quick as he slid the last eight feet at the bottom of the hill.

Shea turned and looked at him, and it was as if time stood still.

"Connor," Shea said, as her breath hung in the air. She looked back at the troll and decided in that split second her course of action.

With all her might, Shea hefted the staff up with both hands grabbing it about a third of the way from the bottom. She put her full weight behind it, spun around and giving the head of the staff some momentum, swung it soundly at the troll...*and missed.*

The troll laughed maniacally as Shea tried to catch herself from going around again. Both hands on the staff, she attempted to balance it evenly across her body, but it continued to pull her downward. A glow from under the ice between Shea and the troll swirled and whipped the currents putting on a frightening display. The ice groaned and crackled in all directions one last time before it gave way beneath her.

Shea plunged into the icy water below but somehow managed to maintain her grip on the staff. The current pulled at her as the staff, now crossways over the hole, kept her from being dragged into the swirling vortex of light. She pulled herself up, getting an elbow over the staff so it rested under her armpit. She sucked in the frigid air, and it burned her lungs. Her hair hung in her face, and the fur cape, now soaking wet, felt as if it weighed a ton.

The current grew stronger, and Shea's grip weakened. She faltered, one shoulder dipping back beneath the water as she knocked her head on the edge of the ice. Dazed, she wrapped her other arm around the staff and waited for the inevitable. It would only be a matter of seconds before the troll got what he came for.

She watched helplessly as the troll walked over to her, standing mere inches from the hole. The light from the dragon's eyes glowed even brighter as he knelt down next to her. She could feel his hot, foul breath on her face and nearly gagged. Her body shivered violently as the cold water took its toll on her. A smile curled the troll's face revealing nasty, rotting teeth, and the black eye gleamed at her as his long fingers wrapped around the staff.

"See you on the other side," he hissed.

Connor rushed out onto the ice diving toward the hole as Shea began to slip under.

"NO!" he shouted, as he slid headfirst at her.

Startled, the troll glared at Connor before releasing his grip on the staff. Throwing himself back away from the hole, the troll disappeared completely.

Laid out flat on the ice, Connor grabbed hold of the staff with both hands, his arms encircling Shea. He found her barely conscious. He could feel her convulsing as the cold wicked its way up through her.

"Hold on," he told her, "I've got you."

Behind him and beneath him, the ice protested even louder under the added weight and the pull from below. Before him, the swirling vortex of light moved toward them against the natural current of the White River. Connor quickly adjusted his arms, moving them under Shea's and pulling himself in close as he gave her an opportunity for one last breath. He held onto the staff for all he was worth and watched the light begin to pull at Shea's feet.

The ice finally gave way and Connor found himself shoulder deep in the water, his head above the surface only by the grace of the staff still miraculously lying crosswise over the hole in the ice. He drew in close behind Shea and lifted her, trying to raise them both up by throwing an elbow over the staff. The ice groaned one last time before giving way completely.

Connor sucked in a final breath just before he, Shea, and the staff were dragged under the frigid water.

In a flash, they were gone.

CHAPTER 13

From their vantage point high in the treetops just on the other side of the boulevard from Oakhurst, Verena and Queen Liliana held each other as they watched the scene breathlessly. Arland grieved in silence with them as they watched the remainder of the drama unfold before their eyes.

The harsh red and blue lights on the emergency rescue vehicles, parked atop the ridge on the opposite side of the river, punctuated the early morning light as workers from the Muncie Fire Department and Delaware County EMS continued to break through the ice on the White River. They had already dragged the stretch between Oakhurst and the falls twice with no results, and the chief had deemed it a recovery mission just before sunrise.

"Maybe they got out," Verena said softly. "Connor is strong. So is Shea....maybe they got out."

Queen Liliana could do nothing but stare at the humans as they talked amongst themselves about how best to proceed. Her heart ached that they did not know how important her son was – *who* he was – or that he was destined to rule a kingdom. Unfamiliar with the ways of humans and how they relate with one another, she could only believe that to them, he was little more than another statistic.

"My Queen, we should go," Arland said. He nodded to the complement behind her. Twenty fae guards stood watch in silence over what remained of the royal family of Oakhurst. The kingdom could not suffer another loss, and they would see to her care. It would become their sole reason for existence in the days to come.

King Rogan and his troops would come. There was nothing holding the inevitable back now.

The Keeper of Time was lost, and so was the Guardian of Oakhurst.

Remnants of Ravensforge

CHAPTER 14

Arland paced before four of his finest of the Guard. The mission ahead of them would be an arduous journey, but if they found what the queen had asked them to find, the benefit would be great for the Kingdom of Oakhurst.

He had chosen three of them, but Queen Liliana had insisted on the fourth, and though he knew not to question her, he was certain there was more to it than most would ever know. He had served her long enough to know that she rarely did anything without thinking it through to five steps beyond the logical conclusion of the situation.

Recognizing that her emotions were still raw at the loss of her son, Arland wondered if Liliana's reasoning may simply be nothing more than an act of self-preservation and the need to put yet another reminder of Connor out of her sight.

Arland stopped and looked them over as all stared straight

ahead. Tristan was the tallest of the group, and his ginger hair and fair complexion made him hard to miss. Finnian and Torin, brothers, both had dark hair and eyes to match that glittered with mischief that seemed to be well contained when the situation called for it. And Caeden, requested by Queen Liliana, whose resemblance to Prince Connor might serve them well should there be trouble on the other end. All looked well-cut and fit for nearly anything, but he knew they may very well fail at the task at hand.

"You have been chosen for this mission because you are adept at traveling in the wilderness. The way will be treacherous and fraught with many dangers, least of which will be the warriors of Hawksgate. You will not, under any circumstances, engage them in battle of any sort. Is that understood?"

"Yes, Master Arland," came their reply in unison.

"You will find the portal to the human realm, and you will report back here at once."

Caeden's gaze snapped at once to Arland, their eyes locked.

"You have a question, Caeden?" the Master asked.

"There is another portal?"

"Yes, there is another portal."

"To what end do we seek this portal? It is not as if Prince Connor can return through it." Caeden stopped short, remembering that the prince had been lost to them.

Arland shot him a look that immediately told him that he'd taken his thinking one step too far.

"You have your orders," Arland barked at them. "Dismissed."

Wet sand stuck to her cheek as Shea awoke to the sounds of the sea rolling in to greet her. She could feel the water lapping at her boots, and her clothes, especially the fur cloak, were soaked and heavy upon her. She was cold, but the sun warmed her as she rolled over onto her back. Unsure of what had happened or how she got there, Shea lay there letting the sun warm her face.

It sounded familiar, like something from her childhood, and she stayed there in a soggy heap for some time taking in the sounds and smells all around.

Her mind wandered aimlessly for but a moment, and when the realization of what had transpired the night before and where she now lay hit her, Shea sat bolt upright on the beach.

Either she was home, or she was dead.

She blinked in the bright sunlight and looked around. It appeared to be the beachhead a short distance from Ravensforge!

Looking down the beach she saw something that startled her. Wherever she was, she was not alone. Sprawled out on the sand further down the beach was Connor. He was not moving, and she scrambled to her feet desperate to get to him.

Her momentum carried her forward for a short distance, then gravity claimed her, and she went tumbling back down into the wet sand. She looked down and realized she was still clutching the staff in her hand and dropped it, managing to get up and run the last short distance to Connor's side.

"Connor," she said breathlessly, as she fell to her knees in the sand. "Connor, wake up."

She shook him and for a moment believed he was not breathing. She placed her face close to his and could feel his breath on her cheek. Relieved, she shook him and he stirred.

"What's for breakfast?" he asked absently.

Shea looked at him dumbfounded, as the memory of their last moments at Oakhurst came flooding back to her. The terrifying sound of the ice breaking beneath them, the cold water pulling them under, the swirling vortex of light, and...*the soulless black eye of the one-eyed troll*.

Something akin to panic caught Shea in the throat, and she shook Connor again, rather violently this time. It was more to make sure he was unharmed than anything, but she needed to know for sure. This might be bad for Shea, but it would be worse – much worse – for Connor.

He stirred on the sand, rolled to his side and opened his eyes, blinking as he looked up at her. She reached out and brushed the sand from his cheek. His skin was damp and cold, and she knew they couldn't stay here long.

"What happened?" he asked, as he propped himself up.

He didn't seem quite right, and Shea watched as he let his head and shoulders drop back down to the sand.

"How do you feel?" she asked, trying not to let her concern overtake her.

"Like I got run over by the grounds keeper's Gator," he joked lamely. "Where are we?"

"I am uncertain," she said, looking around and gauging the situation, "but I believe we are no longer in the human realm. I believe...we are *home*."

ꙮ   ꙮ

Caeden lagged behind a bit watching his traveling companions as they moved to the edges of the Kingdom of Oakhurst. It would be a long journey, and though he was used to traveling with Connor, he knew that would likely never happen again.

It was bad enough that he was responsible for letting the prince cross over to the human realm by way of dark magic. And though in all reality he would not have been able to stop Connor from doing as he pleased, a more experienced Guardian would have taken a more assertive tack.

Truth be told, Caeden had been selected and trained as Connor's Guardian for one reason – he favored the prince in both look and build. He didn't mind serving as a royal decoy. It was an honor, really, but it did come with some pitfalls, the least of which was the fact that the prince tended to take care of Caeden more than Caeden took care of him. Connor watched over him like he would a younger brother.

The day at Ravensforge came to mind. As they walked amidst the rubble of what had been a mighty fortress only days before, Connor held his feelings in check. Caeden's, however, were all over his face. A mask of horror and grief intertwined with a *what-the-hell?* sort of look that he just couldn't manage to keep from escaping his mind to his face in an instant. Connor knew he wouldn't last long and had mercifully released him from the task of walking through the rubble and corpses before them.

Whether it was a need to make up for past shortcomings or assuage some sort of guilt, Caeden couldn't be certain. But he knew it was imperative that he return from this mission with something the queen wanted, if only to prove himself.

A chill wind bit at Caeden, and he pulled the traveling

cloak in close around him.

"Hey, you coming?" Finn called over his shoulder.

Caeden looked up and realized that he'd fallen further behind than he'd intended. Torin and Tristan stopped and waited as he trotted along.

"Sorry," he said.

"Don't want to lose you too early out," Tristan told him.

"No, you needn't worry about that," Caeden told him. "I'm in it for the long haul."

॥ ॥

Shea managed to gather up just enough twigs and brush to make a small fire in an alcove a short distance away. It was protected from the wind, and the sun would continue to warm the spot for some time before it was swallowed up by the shadows.

Stripped down to their breeches and undershirts, Shea and Connor hung their clothes nearby to dry as they warmed themselves at the fire. It would be cold by nightfall and wet clothes would surely be most unpleasant.

"This troll," Shea asked finally, "is he the one you dealt with? The one who sent you to find me?"

Connor's face flushed and eyes down, he continued to watch the fire. He took some time to gather his thoughts before he spoke. "Yes, he is the one."

"He looks...evil. Scary. Like someone you wouldn't ordinarily associate with. His eye was like none I have ever seen before."

"He didn't look like that when I met him. Sure, he only had one eye, but it was no different than yours or mine."

110

Connor looked up at her. "Someone must have gotten to him."

Shea's gut twisted as she mulled over what had to happen. It would be arduous, difficult, and dangerous, and she could not ask Connor to go with her. She poked at the fire with a stick and put the last of the kindling on it.

"He stole the Keeper of Time," she said, "and I have to find him."

"We must travel to Oakhurst. Mother and Arland will have a plan."

"*Your* mother and Arland will wring our necks. Or mine, anyway."

Connor chuckled in spite of their predicament. "She likes you. In her own way."

Shea let the idea of the irony of Connor's statement roll around in her head a bit before she spoke. She decided to measure her words carefully when speaking of the queen for fear she might reveal too much.

"Which is miniscule when measured by others outside the palace walls," she said finally.

"You are thinking in human terms," Connor chided her playfully. "Now you have to think like a faerie again."

"Connor, we cannot go to Oakhurst." She paused. "Let me rephrase that. You can go to Oakhurst. I cannot."

"And why not?"

"Because," Shea said, tempted to tell him the truth. But they were back in the fae realm, and the game had changed dramatically. Her role had transformed in a flash, and she was now honor-bound to recover what had been stolen from her – from all of them. She decided, instead, to err on the side of caution for the time being when it came to sharing Queen Liliana's secrets with her son.

"If I do, if I show up and admit that the Keeper of Time has been stolen out from under our noses, we will have a war on our hands. And I, for one, do not want to be responsible for giving Rogan an excuse to go to war."

Connor sighed heavily, knowing she was right.

"We don't have much time," Shea added gravely, gazing into his eyes. The look on his face confirmed what she felt in her gut about the urgency of finding the Keeper of Time and returning him to the human realm.

"Then we need to go troll hunting," Connor told her, "and I'm afraid I know just where to look."

ᛞ   ᛒ

The midday sun was warm on their backs as Shea and Connor came upon what was left of Castle Ravensforge. Shea's heart sank at the pile of rubble left where her home had once been, and the very sight of it sucked the breath out of her.

She appreciated Connor's distance as they walked amongst the ruins. One touch of his hand, one look with even the slightest hint of unintended pity would bring her crashing down inside. She could not afford that. Not now. Time was not a luxury they had, and Connor's life depended on her. She would not lose him. Dark magic be damned, she would not let that happen.

"We escaped through the catacombs," she recalled aloud. "On that night, the king, he seemed more concerned about the amulet and its safety than that of his own family. He saw to it that everyone was under adequate guard and would be watched over, but the amulet was his first priority as the enemy lay siege upon the castle."

"It must be very powerful," Connor replied, taking care as he stepped over the rocks in his path.

"I can only imagine," Shea answered. "I wish it had come with an instruction manual."

Connor laughed. "Lucy would have appreciated that."

"True," Shea smiled weakly, as she looked around them.

There was nothing left there for her, not anymore. Nothing but painful memories of that final night, but still Shea lingered. She knew it was time to move on, but she desperately longed to know what happened to her family and comrades. *Surely not knowing was worse than having the truth, was it not?*

It was Connor who finally spoke up.

"Shea, we have to go."

CHAPTER 15

Shea saw him from the time they cleared the trees just beyond what had once been the walls of Castle Ravensforge. A lone raven with an enormous wingspan soared high above them regarding their every move. Watching the skies, she and Connor crossed the greensward in silence, moving ever closer toward the sea.

Shea's stomach churned as they neared the cliffs fearing what they might find. The ground was barren and charred, and what was left of those who had fought so valiantly defending her king and queen had long since been picked clean or carried off by various predators. The wind whipped at her cape and hair, smelling more like the fresh sea mists of her childhood than of the death and destruction that had occurred there only a short time ago.

"Maybe they weren't here," Connor offered, as he looked

115

past her toward the sea.

Shea shook her head solemnly. "They were here. If the king was here, they were here. All of them."

Connor avoided her eyes, saying nothing for a great while. Finally, after he thought she'd been there too long, he broke the silence. "Shea, it'll be dark soon. We need to move on."

She nodded, then turned and headed along the edge of the cliff.

"Where are you going?"

"Following him," she called over her shoulder.

"Following? Who?"

He watched as Shea pointed skyward at the raven, fresh off his perch and moving swiftly in the opposite direction of the setting sun.

"Well, where is he going?" Connor asked, glancing back at the sun as it began its descent into night.

"To the Forge."

ᛞᚩ   ᚳᛂ

Grief-stricken, Verena sat in the colonnade garden and sobbed. To lose Royce had been bad enough. But to have her brother, even in his human form, ripped away from them was more than she could bear. Her favorite place in the gardens had become her self-imposed prison as she could scarcely stand to be in the presence of others any longer.

It wasn't their actions or words but their thoughts that hurt her deeply. Not those of condolence or sadness but the pity that the princess had suffered two losses in such a short time. None of them realized that pity is such a waste of energy, good for neither side of the transaction. And one thing she refused to do was pity herself, for that was the worst of all.

If there was anything beyond trusting her instincts that her father taught her, it was that in order to handle a bad situation in life, one must take action. King Marco had always been a man of action, and right or wrong, Verena had admired that quality in him most of all.

Her mother had it as well. She would not have been such a good ruler of the kingdom had she not been of that mindset. She made decisions and stuck with them, remaining steadfast and consistent with those whom she ruled over.

That was not to say that the queen had not made a bad choice of actions in her past. That, to Verena, was very apparent when her mother spoke of certain things. But the two of them had never discussed it for the simple fact that Verena knew that her mother's mistakes, though made long ago, still pained her greatly to this day.

Drying her eyes, Verena stood and brushed herself off. Determination written all over her face, she set off to find the one being in the garden who might be able to help her find the answers she sought.

But she would have to do it in stealth, for she knew without a doubt that her mother would not approve.

      ഌ   ഐ

Torin, Finn, and Tristan joined Caeden on the ridge. From there they could see land that stretched for what seemed like eternity. It was a warm, golden-colored terrain, mostly flat with only a few places that might cause them trouble.

"Do you really know where we're going?" Finn asked Caeden skeptically.

"It is a difficult task to find a hidden people that do not wish to be found," Caeden answered. "We go north. When we run out of north, we will have found them."

"That's all you've got?" Torin chided him.

"I'm afraid so."

"Where'd you get those bloody directions?" Tristan grumbled.

"Arland. But we needn't go all the way to Hawksgate," Caeden reminded them. "Only to the portal."

"And then?" Finn asked.

Caeden raised an eyebrow and grinned.

"We go through."

ಬ   ೞ

"I was here long ago," Shea told Connor. Short of breath from the climb, she longed to rest but instead pressed on. It would be dark soon, and she knew that it would be too dangerous to remain on the bluffs. "My father brought me here as a child."

"Do you know what you're looking for exactly?" he inquired. "I see nothing here."

"Honestly, I don't remember seeing the doorway to the Forge until we were right on top of it. My father told me it was a secret, known only to the Guard."

"And do you know this secret?"

Shea stopped a few feet ahead of him, turning to look past Connor at the sun sinking behind him. She was as unsure of whether she could find it as he was, and though she wanted to reassure him, she had nothing to offer him but words. Empty words. She leaned on the Dragon Staff, shaking her head.

118

Her heart ached as she thought again of her father. He would have died before he let anything happen to the king, and if Darius Pendragon had been as powerful in this realm as he was in the human realm, she knew her father would not have stood a chance without the aid of the relics. They were the only thing that had kept Shea alive in the battle at Oakhurst, and she knew it.

Turning back to the slope, she scanned the hillside in the late afternoon light. It was hopeless, and she was nearly ready to suggest they head back down when she spotted it. It was covered in a tangle of vines, but the door was visible nonetheless.

"There!" she cried. "Do you see it?"

"Where? No…"

Shea quickened her pace up the incline using the staff to steady her steps as she made good progress. She could hear Connor behind her but was afraid to take her eyes off the door for fear she'd lose it in the coming darkness.

A good twenty steps ahead of him, she came to a stop in front of the huge wooden double doors. Hand-hewn, they were bound with hammered black iron and black nails with large, round black door pulls to match.

"Where is it, Shea?" Connor asked, as he pulled up short right behind her. Out of breath, he doubled over.

"Connor, really," Shea asked, thinking he was teasing. She turned to find him looking slightly paled. "Are you all right?"

"I'll be fine," he said, straightening up. "Now, where's this door?"

"Connor, it's *right here*," she said somewhat harshly, placing her hand on the door pull.

The look on Connor's face told her the truth – *he couldn't see the doorway to the Forge!* She looked back at it. It still looked the same as it had before, only now Connor could see it as well.

"I swear to you on my mother's crown, it wasn't there an instant ago."

℘ ℂ

It had been a long journey, and Caeden was beginning to believe it was a futile one. The terrain looked the same in every direction, and perhaps that was the beauty and genius in the camouflage of Hawksgate. Much like the feathers of the hawk hide it among the branches from below so, too, the Kingdom of Hawksgate was hidden from view of outsiders. For all Caeden knew, they might have walked past it by now.

And Arland's rather ambiguous directions didn't help the cause much either.

Caeden had listened to Finn, Torin, and Tristan grumble for the last half day and hoped they would find the portal soon if only to assuage their complaining. It wasn't the mission as much as the method that had disgruntled them so. He wasn't quite sure what they had expected, but he knew that the next leg of the journey would certainly surprise them.

In the lead, Finn stopped suddenly raising his hand for quiet.

"What is it?" Tristan asked quietly.

Finn's response was to hold a finger to his lips with one hand as he drew his sword with the other. Taking their cue from him, the others followed suit and listened intently.

It took a moment before Caeden heard it, too. A rustling in the brush some distance away but distinctly moving in their direction. *Fast*. Caeden looked back at Finn trying to read his face for some sense of what to do next.

A huge shadow passed over them, and Caeden looked upward just missing sight of what it was. Finn, noting the shadow as well, knew there was nothing they could do here.

"Run!" Finn ordered them.

The foursome sprinted in the opposite direction of the noise. What happened next increased their desire to flee as well as their speed.

A sharp cry from overhead followed by a thrashing and screeching in the woods behind them propelled them forward. The branches and vines whipped at them as they tore through the thicket. Swords still in hand, they hacked at them as best they could but could still not escape the sting of the branches against their faces.

Tired of fighting with it, Caeden put his sword back in the sheath and did his best to push the branches out of the way with his hands. The noises behind them had died down, but without knowing exactly what the threat was, he knew it unwise to stop so soon. They pushed onward.

A short distance ahead of him he could see open sky and was relieved they would soon be beyond the tree line where they might at least be able to see what was coming at them.

Caeden emerged from the trees first and, eyes forward, did not see the slope before him that dropped off sharply. He noticed just in time, tried his best to stop, but his heels and momentum dragged him to the edge. Gravity finished the job, dragging him downward just after his heels cleared the edge of the bluff. He took quite a tumble and a great deal of loose rock and debris with him.

Tristan pulled up just short of the edge managing not to

follow suit with Torin and Finn barreling in right behind him. Tristan stretched out his arms to try to keep the other two from going over and closed his eyes as he braced for impact from behind. The brothers somehow managed to stop just in time

Relieved, Tristan opened his eyes. Taking a cautious look over the edge, he could see Caeden in a crumpled heap at the bottom of the slope.

"Caeden!" he called. "Are you all right?"

On the ground beneath them Caeden stirred. Scraped and battered beyond belief, the traveling cloak wrapped around him like a burial cloth, he struggled a moment to untangle himself.

"Yes, yes, I am fine," he grumbled loudly, as he looked around to find his bearings. He was feeling quite put out at the whole tumble when his eyes lit up.

"Finn?" he hollered up.

"Yes?"

"You need to get down here."

"Letting your resemblance to a certain prince get the best of you? Order us around, will you?" Finn teased. "Don't let that go to your head now."

"I think you'll want to see this," Caeden shouted back.

"And why is that?"

"Because I believe our search is over."

૪૦   ૦૩

Shea took hold of the iron handle on the great door of the Forge. Feeling the cold metal against her skin, she hesitated. It sent a chill through her as she thought of what might be waiting for them behind that door. Her greatest fear was that

122

there would be no one there tending the fires. No one there hammering the steel. No one left to balance the weapons. Her greatest fear was that the Forge would be nothing more than a hollow, secret chamber in the side of the mountain.

She looked back at Connor, took in a deep breath and heaved herself backwards, giving the door hanger a mighty pull.

The heavy wooden door groaned in protest as if it had not been opened for centuries. Dust and pebbles rained down on them from the cliff face above, and they took cover in the anteroom of the Forge. In the waning daylight the raven called to them one last time before taking leave of them. Silently, Connor pulled the door shut behind them.

Both were aware of the reverence this place held. To become a Swordsmith was one of the highest callings in the Kingdom of Ravensforge, second only to that of Guardian to the royals. The Master Swordsmith answered directly to the king himself.

The heat grew as they made their way into the main hall of the Forge. It was cavernous, and the torches lining the hall kept the room well-lit. Several waist-high benches made of stone formed a circle, each facing the forge in the front of the room. The embers glowed as if awaiting the Master Swordsmith's return.

At the far end of the main hall stood the armory. It was a beautifully carved wooden case that was half as wide as the hall and went nearly all the way to the ceiling. Designed to hold at least a hundred swords, it stood empty, save for three weapons hanging on the very top row. In the middle was a ladder which was attached at the top and made to slide along the length of the case. Shea and Connor approached it, speaking in hushed tones.

"Looks like the arsenal has been cleaned out," Connor noted, while taking hold of the ladder. He eased it along the case until it reached the remaining weapons. He brought it to a stop then climbed upward until he could almost touch the ceiling. His stomach turned as he thought of what had happened to the sword that had been given to him by King Beltran. He reached out to remove one of the remaining swords from the wall.

"Connor, I don't think –" Shea began.

Connor stayed his hand and looked down at her. He had grown to respect her judgment. "Just a closer look," he called back down to her.

Taking great care with them, he escorted the swords one by one down the ladder placing each on the bench closest to the case that had been covered with a luxurious, purple velveteen cloth. Ceremonial in purpose, it was apparent that it had been set aside for the king's viewing pleasure.

Shea stepped over to inspect the weapons as Connor placed the last of them on the table. They were magnificent as the firelight from the torches danced along the length of each blade. The ruby eyes of the ravens that made up the hilt glistened, beckoning Connor to pick them up again.

He relished the feel of the sword in his hand. It was perfect. Its craftsmanship, rumored to be unmatched in the realm, was impeccable, and he could see why King Beltran had been so proud to give him the Sword of Nobility to bind the deal of his intention to betroth one of the daughters of Ravensforge.

It was probably just as well that the king didn't know what Connor had done with it. Beltran would surely roll in his grave at the thought of the one-eyed troll even laying hands on it. Truly, it would be akin to betrothing one of his daughters to the foul troll. Connor shivered at the thought.

"Magnificent," Connor said, as he stood over the swords and admired them in the torchlight.

He looked to Shea who nodded in agreement. He could see in her eyes the power and importance of the Forge to her people and knew this was a reverent place for her. Gently, he placed the sword back on the velveteen cloth on top of the table taking a step back.

"A blade fit for service to a king."

ᛒ ᛦ

Apprehension rose as he watched from the recesses of the Forge, waiting for them to leave. They stood examining the blades in quiet tones for longer than he would have liked and was relieved when the weapons were back on the table and out of their hands.

Still uncertain of how they were able to enter the Forge in the first place, he knew his duty was clear – protect the swords at all costs until King Beltran's return. Though they did not appear to be of the Dark Warrior's ranks, nor his minions, they could not be trusted.

He would stand his post to the last. The remaining three swords created by the Master Swordsmith himself awaited the king's blessing, and he swore he would not let him down. However, he would not be able to wait out these interlopers.

If need be, he would dispatch them himself.

Chapter 16

Shea could feel eyes on the back of her neck. She wasn't sure how long they had been under surveillance, only that they were being watched, and she didn't like it in the least.

"Oh, *Connor*," she called across the room in a rather odd tone, "perhaps we should leave this place."

"But why?" the prince asked, barely looking up from the various tools on the stone bench before him. "It has grown dark outside. There is obviously no one here so why not just stay? We'll get a fresh start in the morning." Connor looked up to see the strangest look on Shea's face. Her stance was steady, but her eyes danced to and fro wildly like she was trying to tell him something.

"*Behind me*," she mouthed silently. *"Behind the stone column to my left."*

"Of...*course*," Connor continued slowly as he moved

toward the forge in an attempt to draw the attention of whomever it was observing them, "we could always backtrack to the cove down slope from here." His steps brought him within reaching distance of the final three swords created in the fires of Ravensforge. "But we must take these beauties with us. It would be a shame for someone to come along and *steal* them."

Locating a sheath nearby, Connor strapped it around his waist and picked up one of the swords. He watched Shea slip silently back toward the stone column in question as he made a rather grand spectacle of himself.

"Perhaps I need two of these, don't you think, Shea?" he teased, as he wielded one in either hand slashing the air first with one, then the other. They were lightweight and perfectly balanced and as truly exquisite as he remembered the Sword of Nobility having been.

Dancing about the chamber in a mock battle with himself, Connor's actions brought the desired response. The spy behind the column could stand his insolence no longer. Blade drawn, a young man barely past his teens stepped out to challenge the prince.

"I'll thank you to put those swords down, sir," said the young man in his bravest tone. He was little more than a boy, and though his voice quivered slightly, he made it perfectly clear with the point of his blade that he was deadly serious.

"And I'll thank you to put down yours," Shea countered quietly, the cool steel of her own blade pressed convincingly against the side of his neck.

The young man raised his arms in surrender as his hand let the sword drop to the stone floor. The steel clattered and echoed in the chamber, protesting loudly as it witnessed the last sentinel of the Forge in apparent defeat.

Shea lowered her blade slightly and stepped away giving the lad room to breathe yet remaining just close enough to discourage any brash ideas he may have.

"Who are you?" she asked.

The boy raised his chin proudly. "I am Prentice, last of the swordsmiths of Ravensforge. I have been sworn to defend the Forge until the Masters' return."

"Where have the Masters gone?" Connor asked.

Astonishment and incredulity shadowed his face as if to silently ask if they were both totally mad. "To battle the Dark Warrior of Erebos. King Beltran had sent word by way of the Guard that the castle was under siege." His eyes narrowed at the strangers in his home. "Who are you to be asking these things?" he demanded, slipping back into his false bravado.

Connor and Shea exchanged glances. It was Shea who answered his question in a quiet voice.

"I am Shea, Guardian of Oakhurst, former Guardian to the daughters of Beltran of Ravensforge. This is Connor, of the Seventh Line of Ashtan, Crown Prince of Oakhurst, and future heir to Beltran's throne."

Prentice's bravado was swiftly replaced with utter shock and mortification as he quickly knelt on the floor before Connor. "A thousand pardons, Your Majesty," he said humbly. "Please forgive me."

Connor raised an eyebrow to Shea as he straightened himself and put on a regal air. "Rise, Prentice of the Forge. Pray, tell us what has happened here."

Prentice rose from the floor and looked around. "This is all that is left. The swords here are all that are left of the craftsmen who toiled here. When word came that Ravensforge

129

was under attack, the Master of the Forge gathered all but a handful of men and took weapons to defend the king and his Guard." His eyes grew cold. "They did not return."

"And the others?" Shea asked, not sure she wanted to know.

"When the Master and his men did not return, everyone here went out to find what had become of them. We could see the fires of Ravensforge burning in the distance. We could hear the Dark Warrior's minions coming in the night. We knew he was coming for us. *For the Forge*. And we knew we could not let that happen."

"So the rest fought him off?" Connor presumed.

"They tried," Prentice replied, "but not before hiding the entrance to the Forge."

"But I saw it plain as day," Shea corrected him.

"How can that be?" Prentice asked, confused. "It has been hidden from the eyes of fae and men alike, apparent only to he who holds the Amulet of Fire."

"Or she," Connor muttered under his breath, shooting Shea a quick glance.

"We got lucky," Shea covered nicely, thankful that the amulet was tucked safely under her breastplate. The fewer fae who knew that she possessed it the better. "Must've been the way the setting sun was shining."

Prentice merely shrugged it off. "So, has King Beltran sent you? What of the Master of the Forge?"

"We're…not sure," Connor began.

"There was a fierce battle," Shea told him. "Many fae were lost."

"And the king?"

"We do not know."

"What of those whom you were sworn to protect? His daughters?"

Shea sighed. They had yet to find the princesses, and she was frustrated by the fact that she didn't even know where to begin to look. "I do not know. They escaped to the human realm but beyond that, I am uncertain. They could be anywhere."

୫୦   ଔ

The portal of Hawksgate stood before them. It looked just like the one Caeden had seen on the edge of the Kingdom of Ravensforge, only this one appeared to be undamaged. With any luck it would be fully functional.

It was a boulder, the face of which had been cut and polished to a smooth sheen. The center of the boulder sparkled a dazzling gold-colored drusy quartz in the late afternoon sun.

Arland had instructed Caeden on how to operate it, and he stepped closer to examine it. He reached out and touched it, and the center of it rippled like water in a still pond.

"Arland said it will not take us to Oakhurst in the human realm," Caeden said as he watched the portal, "but it will take us somewhere human."

"And from there?" Torin asked.

"We find the princesses of Ravensforge."

The other three began to move in toward him. Caeden turned to find all three of them looking skyward with horrified looks on their faces. Simultaneously they drew their swords, but somehow Caeden knew it would be useless against whatever was bearing down on them. Alarmed, he turned his face up just in time to see talons bearing down upon him. All

131

he could do was raise his arms to cover his head in a feeble attempt to protect himself.

The sharp claws grabbed his arms, snatching Caeden off the ground and dragging him upward at a phenomenal rate. He hadn't even had the sense to scream but knew this was probably the end for him.

Just as well, really, he thought to himself.

At least there would be someone left to tell his tale and make one final excuse for his failure to the queen.

ଧ   ଓ

"Oh, bloody hell," Tristan complained, as he watched the giant hawk take Caeden higher and higher.

"Let's go," Torin said, "before he becomes dessert."

The three took off after the bird at a dead run. Glancing back and forth from where the hawk was flying to the direction they were running and back again, they followed as best they could but knew they would not be able to keep up that pace for long. They were still spent from fleeing what had presumably been the same hawk just before it had enjoyed its dinner.

With any luck, it wouldn't be hungry and might save Caeden for later.

Worse yet, they would soon run out of daylight.

ଧ   ଓ

Caeden fought and struggled as best he could, but the hawk's grip only tightened on his arms. Mercifully, the sharp claws had missed piercing his skin and he was grateful for that

132

slight at least for the moment.

His futile attempts to free himself exhausted, Caeden resorted to the only tool left to him: he screamed, loud and long. Hoping to frighten the bird or at least temporarily startle it, he wiggled and kicked and screamed at the top of his lungs.

"Aye! Quiet down a bit, your princely-ness!" came a loud voice from above him.

Startled, Caeden stopped screaming and looked up. Peering around the neck of the hawk that had captured him was a fae, his wild hair blowing in the breeze.

Taken somewhat aback, Caeden took a different tack.

"You will put me down," he ordered the fae. *"NOW!"*

"Oh, I think not, your lordship," the fae replied in earnest.

"Where are we going?" Caeden asked. "Surely you can at least tell me that."

"Of course," the fae answered back. "We're going to Hawksgate."

"Well, that tears it," Caeden muttered to himself. His arms were growing numb from the hawk's grip on them and the awkward position they were trapped in. "I don't suppose you could do anything about my arms?" he called up to the fae on hawkback. "I'm afraid they've fallen asleep."

"How could they with a view like this?" the fae kidded him.

"I don't think they much care about the view."

"Alright, hold on a minute," the fae called back down to him. "Brace yourself."

"For *what?!*" Caeden squawked, his alarm most apparent in the question.

As if in response to his answer Caeden felt himself propelled forward by the hawk's strong legs just before the talons released him. His legs led him upward and his torso had no recourse but to follow as the momentum sent him into an awkward, sprawling backward flip. He screamed even louder as his arms flailed wildly.

Caeden found himself staring at the ground as it moved up toward him at an alarming rate. Head first he plummeted toward the earth wishing with all his might that he were in the human realm. At least there he had wings with which to flee.

He closed his eyes tight and covered his head with his arms as he braced for the horrible impact that would follow his rapid descent. Just shy of the treetops he felt the hawk once again take hold of him, grabbing up his legs and making for an even more uncomfortable flight.

From above, the fae looked down at Caeden.

"Awwwwhh," he groaned, "that's not right. Aswynn, again, if you please."

Aswynn the hawk gave a sharp cry and once again flung Caeden forward sending him flailing yet again through the air. This time she caught him upright by the shoulders and for that Caeden was most grateful.

"Thank you," he breathed, as relief washed over him.

The view of the setting sun was truly spectacular, and now that he was somewhat assured that he would not be the hawk's evening meal, Caeden could almost relax. But he knew that it would take a divine act of diplomacy to get him out of this one. Encroaching on another kingdom's portal was frowned upon and could conceivably be viewed as an act of war if handled improperly.

Caeden hoped he would be able to handle it properly.

CHAPTER 17

Connor awoke before Shea and Prentice and went out into the main hall of the Forge alone. He could understand why the Guard of Ravensforge had held it in such esteem. It was a place of incredible potential in terms of craftsmanship and what it meant for the kingdom. Peace through strength, something that Beltran had prided himself on and was known for throughout the realm.

Connor's thoughts turned to what it might have been like if he were to rule over Ravensforge. Nothing more than a mental exercise now, but he and Beltran were very different. His mother, though guarded with her words when it came to affairs of state, sometimes let it slip what she truly thought of others in the royal ranks.

While the queen held Beltran in high esteem, Connor sensed that she thought him somewhat braggadocios where the Keeper of Time was concerned. After all, without the stones from Elisabeth's mother's earrings, the relic was nothing more than a worthless piece of incomplete art.

But what perplexed him was the fact that Beltran, in all his pride, managed to keep the Amulet of Fire a secret. In conversations around the fire before he and Caeden had departed, Connor heard his mother speak of it in hushed tones to Arland and a handful of trusted advisors, most of whom were well-versed in the old ways and had an understanding of both light and dark magic.

Connor warmed himself by the forge. The embers glowed warmly and brought him a sense of comfort. His thoughts turned to what lie ahead for them, and he felt himself shudder involuntarily. It would not be pleasant.

His hands ached in the joints as he opened and closed them several times to loosen them up a bit. He turned his palms over, noting that his knuckles were slightly swollen.

So it begins, he thought to himself.

The dark magic had taken its hold on him once again.

ᛞ   ങ

Verena left her quarters in the early morning light, moving stealthily along the corridor of her family's palace. Uncertain of how long she might be or even if she would return, she cast a long glance back over her shoulder before stepping out the door into the treetops of Oakhurst Gardens.

Slipping past Rayne would be the most difficult task. It was as if she sensed when Verena was ready to move and would suddenly appear out of thin air. Nonetheless, Rayne could not go where Verena planned to go.

It would be a struggle to find them, but she knew if there

were even the remotest of chances that they might be found, she could not simply sit back and wait for them to return. If they could have, they would. It was now up to her, Verena told herself.

She had hidden the magic box away for the protection of everyone around her. Though her mother had ordered the box destroyed, Verena could not bear to even think of that happening with her beloved Royce inside. Yes, they would be ridding the realm of the scourge that were the Gutiku, but it was a magic that she had yet to understand fully.

She could sense that it was a different sort of magic and had been able to since the day she and Royce had discovered it. Even before she had made the mistake of opening it, she could feel the co-mingling of light and dark magic from within.

Bearing a heavy burden of culpability in the matter, Verena could not help but wonder how things might have turned out had she not opened the magic box in the first place. Royce would still be here. Probably Connor and Shea as well. And though Verena knew exactly how her mother felt about Shea and her budding relationship with Connor, she did not wish her ill will. Neither of them did, for that matter.

But Verena did know to what lengths one would go to for love. Fighting with that side of herself since the day Royce was sucked into the box, she knew that her line of thinking was not rational. She knew that her fondest hope was utterly impossible. And she knew that she would not let any of the three of them go if there were even the slightest chance that she might be able to bring them home safely.

So desperate was she to be held in his arms again, she would even settle for Royce in human form and would gladly go wherever he was just to be with him.

Verena hated the thought of leaving her mother all alone. She, too, had suffered a great loss that began with her father and ended when Connor disappeared. Arland would watch over her and that brought some sense of comfort to the princess.

That would have to be enough.

ɞ ʓ

Torin stood watch in the early morning light as Tristan doused what was left of the fire. Finn stretched and packed up the last of their belongings as they made ready to depart.

"Any idea of how far out we are?" Finn asked, as Tristan sniffed at the air.

"Hard to say," Tristan replied. "But I'd wager we're closer than you think."

"How do you know this?" Torin called to him as he moved in closer to the fire.

"Them," Tristan said calmly, nodding toward the detachment of guards that surrounded them. "Bet they'll show us how to get there."

ɞ ʓ

"What of your journey?" Prentice asked them over a modest breakfast of dried bread and jam. "Where do you intend to go?"

Shea looked at Connor not wanting to share too much but feeling the need to tell Prentice something.

"To Erebos," Shea said matter-of-factly before taking

138

another bite of bread.

Prentice nearly choked.

"Erebos? Surely you cannot be serious."

"I am afraid we are," Connor answered for her. "We are on a mission of grave importance, one that will affect both our realm and that of the humans."

"Humans? Rubbish!" Prentice scoffed. "Nothing more than children's stories."

Shea and Connor looked at him in earnest, and their expressions spoke volumes.

"You've seen them?" Prentice asked. "Truly, you've seen them?"

"More than that," Shea answered. "We've been there."

"On your honor?" he inquired in disbelief.

"On my honor as Guardian of the daughters of the House of Beltran," Shea replied. "I have walked among them."

"Are they as sly and mischievous as we were told as children?" the young one quizzed her.

"Actually," she replied, "they are more like us than you could possibly imagine."

ଥ   ଓ

Caeden awoke in the most comfortable bed he'd ever slept in. Though his eyes were still closed, he lie there thinking of what was in store for him on this day. And then it hit him: he was not at Oakhurst but a prisoner in the palace of Hawksgate! Startled at the revelation in his mind, he sat bolt upright in bed.

He looked around the room taking in the opulence of it all, from the beautiful chandelier hanging from the ceiling to the stunning view out the window to the plush blankets that covered him. The prior evening's events came flooding back to him. And while he knew Queen Liliana would frown upon his actions, he saw no other recourse than to simply follow along and see where it led him.

Quietly he slipped from underneath the covers, and his bare feet padded across the floor to the door. He opened it, just a crack, to peer out into the corridor. Two guards stood steadfast at their post seemingly ignoring him and his curiosity. Caeden said nothing and closed the door.

Taken with the view, he walked to the window. A tray with his breakfast – a rather hearty one at that – sat on a small table next to the window. His stomach growled at the aroma of the food, but his head would not allow him to enjoy the meal. He stared out the window and wondered what had happened to his traveling companions and hoped they had at least had the good sense to escape through the portal. Perhaps they would be able to find the princesses on their own. He could only hope they wouldn't get too distracted by the humans and their lifestyle.

The door behind him swung inward and Caeden turned to find a noble of sorts standing there escorted by the two guards from the corridor.

"If you please, Your Highness," the noble said. "King Astor will see you now."

৯০ ০৪

Prentice shared what little supplies he had left with them, and Connor threw the rucksack over his shoulder as they set out in search of the Keeper of Time. Shea bid him farewell,

140

reminding him to lock the door behind them. Though she was not sure what good it would do, it seemed like the sensible thing to say.

The early morning light was soothing somehow, and they made their way down the mountain in silence, both knowing that the journey ahead of them would be difficult. The troll already had a half-day's start on them, and though they had their suspicions as to where he was, it was a guess more than an exact science.

Shea knew the terrain of the Kingdom of Ravensforge quite well, as it came with the territory of protecting the King and his family. She had also been taught well in terms of the surrounding kingdoms and how to get to and from them. But like a teenager with a new license to drive, she knew she had to get somewhere but wasn't quite sure how to go about it.

Erebos was more legend in the fae realm than a place one might visit, and she wondered if they didn't just prefer to keep it that way out of a false sense of security rather than learning how to protect themselves from the forces that resided there. It was one thing to tell tales about it but something totally different when it came to actually going there – to face whatever lie within. And that would not be fun at all.

Shea watched Connor as he walked ahead of her. Outwardly he seemed fine, and she wanted to keep it that way for as long as possible. She did not know what effects the remnants of the dark magic might bring down upon him, and she hoped they wouldn't be there long enough to find out. Then again, she wasn't sure how long it would take for things to go south for him. They would just have to wait it out.

She couldn't bear the thought of losing him. They had grown close over the past months they'd spent together, and

141

truthfully, she was growing quite accustomed to the life they were building together. Shea knew the queen would never accept her, and she was fine with that notion so long as she had dealings with her between realms and not within the same one.

She chuckled to herself at the thought of Queen Liliana crossing into the human realm. However, the image turned ugly as she imagined the ruler of Oakhurst coming and killing her in her sleep to be rid of her once and for all. Ludicrous, she knew, but it still might be a possibility.

"Hey, slow-poke, get a move on," Connor called from a good ways ahead of her.

Startled at the distance that had grown between them in the short time she'd been daydreaming, Shea trotted to catch up. Short of breath, she pulled up short beside him.

"Where were you?" he asked.

"Oakhurst. Your mother had crossed over to the human realm and killed me as I slept. Apparently my mind agrees on some level that she does not approve."

"*Ooohhh,*" Connor responded, his eyes wide and mocking, "like that'll ever happen."

"Not the human type?"

"She did that once…with disastrous results."

CHAPTER 18

The noble led Caeden through the fabulous corridors of Hawksgate to the throne room. He did not have to look backward to know that the two guards behind him had been joined by a full detachment of the Guard. He chuckled to himself knowing he was in quite a pickle and that he had no idea how he would extricate himself from the situation. Arland had failed to train him for this.

It appeared, however, that the Guard of Hawksgate didn't know that.

Fae lined the walls of the throne room six deep from back to front, and Caeden was escorted up the long red carpet to the throne where King Astor was seated.

He was a handsome man; his dark eyes and black hair with wisps of silver running back from his face reflected a sense of inner wisdom. He was leaning to one side, his goateed chin resting calmly on his palm.

The king studied the young fae being brought before him quietly.

"Your Majesty," the noble declared, as he came to a stop and bowed low before the throne, "may I present to you Connor, of the Seventh Line of Ashtan, Crown Prince of Oakhurst."

Well, that tears it, Caeden thought to himself. *The queen will surely have my head.*

"So," King Astor said slowly, as he straightened himself on his throne. He looked the faux prince up and down. "This is the one who would court and marry one of my granddaughters?"

Though he tried to rein it in before speaking, surprise registered on Caeden's face. The fact that King Astor was the father of Queen Astra of Ravensforge had completely slipped his mind. Quite cognizant of the crowd around him, he knew that he had to pull this off properly should he ever hope to see Oakhurst again.

The king raised an eyebrow at the pregnant pause that hung between them. "Well?"

"Your Majesty, if I may," Caeden began. The king nodded and he continued. "I have come seeking your assistance. We have word from a reliable source that your granddaughters escaped to the human realm through the portal at Ravensforge."

"A reliable source?" the king asked hopefully. "Who?"

Caeden raised his chin. "Shea of Ravensforge, Guardian of the daughters of Beltran."

"This Guardian failed the task of keeping the princesses safe," King Astor contended. "What makes her such a reliable source?"

144

“I have seen her in action. She is of good and true character,” Caeden vouched for her. “She has fought the minions of the Dark Messenger of Erebos and tamed a dragon in the human realm.”

Astor raised his eyebrows in astonishment. “This one who is now Guardian of Oakhurst is the one who stood guard over my granddaughters? The one who *lost* them?” Incredulity clouded his expression, and Caeden could tell the king struggled with his admiration for the girl-warrior and his frustration at her failure to protect the princesses.

Taking care with his words, Caeden proceeded slowly. “Through no fault of her own. They were being pursued by the Dark Messenger of Erebos and a horde of minions.” He paused, registering the king’s response. “She was the reason they were able to escape.”

“Then I must meet with this one to thank her properly.”

Caeden sighed deeply at the king’s words. “I am afraid that is not possible,” he said solemnly. “The Guardian is missing.”

ꕤ ꕤ

It was a cold journey from the treetop palace of Oakhurst to the river’s bend. The ice had been broken away in the search for Connor and Shea, and the frigid waters flowed freely below Verena as she flew just above the river. She had done a bit of investigating with some rather unsavory characters in the outlying sprite settlements but felt that it would be worth it. They all directed her to the one who would be able to help her in her quest.

Though they cared little whether the Prince of Nebosham

ever returned, or who she was for that matter, she was kind in her dealings with them and they wished her well in her endeavors in return.

They had warned her, however, that she was headed for trouble. "What's a nice girl like you looking for *her* for?" they would scold. Verena could sense no ill-will toward her but still kept her plans to herself.

Lighting atop the concrete abutment beneath the midpoint of the bridge on Wheeling Avenue, Verena made her way up into the steel under-structure of the bridge. Three quarters of the way to the other side she found what she was looking for – a hole in the concrete no bigger than what the humans called a quarter.

Squeezing through the opening, she found a long corridor that was surprisingly well-lit. Cautiously she moved along in silence. At the end was a door.

Verena opened it slowly, peering into the room. "Hello?" she called. "Is anyone here?" No one answered, and she stepped inside.

Cupboards and shelves lined the walls in the dimly-lit room. She looked around at the variety of boxes, jars, and trinkets on the shelves. A strange selection of unusual animal pelts hung from the ceiling, and Verena started to think this was a bad idea.

"Looking for me?" came a voice from the doorway behind her. "Just make yourself at *home*, why don't you?"

Startled, Verena wheeled about on her heels. *She hadn't even sensed her approach!*

"I – uh, I am Verena," she said, gathering her composure, acting braver than she felt, "Princess of Oakhurst. I come seeking your help."

146

The pixie made her way into the room. She was petite, with short, fiery red hair and brilliant emerald eyes that flashed at her unexpected guest. Childlike she walked boldly to Verena and looking up at her demanded one thing.

"Get *out*."

Not used to being spoken to in that manner, Verena was taken aback. "I – I'm sorry? What did you say?"

"I said," the pixie repeated, "get *OUT!*" She shoved Verena soundly, knocking her against the shelves behind her. Trinkets and bottles spilled off the shelves and onto the floor, making a horrible racket.

"Please, you don't understand!" Verena cried. "I've come because I need your help!"

"Since *when?!*" the pixie asked angrily. "Since *when* does a *faerie* need anything from a *pixie?*"

Verena sighed, knowing exactly what the pixie was talking about.

"Since my brother has gone missing," Verena told her, "and so has Royce."

ॐ   ॐ

"Missing?" King Astor inquired. "What do you mean, 'missing'?"

Caeden knew that he had to mind his words. One mention of 'himself' in third person would blow the whole thing skyward.

"In her post as Guardian of Oakhurst, Shea of Ravensforge was overcome by forces yet unknown to us." Caeden shifted slightly, allowing his mind time enough to formulate the portion of the story that was not quite completely true. "She

147

sincerely wished to find your granddaughters. However, she is gone now. Since she is unable to complete the task of finding them, that duty, as future husband to one of the daughters of Beltran, falls to me."

King Astor brightened, as if struck with a brilliant idea. He seemed impressed with the younger fae's pluck, and in that moment resolved to help in any way he could.

"Very well, Prince Connor of Oakhurst," the king said. "The resources of my kingdom are at your disposal."

Caeden smiled in spite of the deceptive nature of his act. *This could work yet.*

"Thank you, Your Majesty," he said. "If we might have use of your portal, I –"

King Astor raised a hand to silence the "prince." "The portal of Hawksgate has not been used since the time before my grandfather. I have guards protecting it to prevent passage from this realm to the next."

"So I've seen," Caeden replied, rubbing his still aching shoulder. "But we are desperate. Your Majesty, I implore you. I can show you how to work it. Together we can find your granddaughters."

"I did not believe in humans until I saw them with my own eyes in the gardens of Oakhurst," Astor said. "I must admit, I find it rather distasteful that my granddaughters are living among them."

"Then you will allow us to pass?" Caeden asked hopefully.

"There are greater implications than you know, my boy," King Astor said. "I will allow you to go through the portal but on one condition."

"Anything, Your Majesty," Caeden agreed, with relief in his voice.

King Astor nodded and smiled. "An audience with your mother for my top advisor to negotiate usage of the portal."

"My – *mother?*" Caeden asked, in disbelief. In his mind's eye he saw it all play out before him in a brief instant, and none of it ended well for the royal decoy. "But King Astor, time is of the essence…"

"And that is why I want to do it right the first time. Because we may only have one chance."

ᛞ   ᛈ

"One chance?" Tristan asked, when he and the others had been retrieved from the dungeon and reunited behind closed doors with their "prince." "What does he mean by that?"

"I don't know," Caeden admitted.

"Bloody likely it's nothing good," Torin added. "You say the king's none the wiser that you're not who he thinks you are."

"So far as I can tell," Caeden said, "but I have to take care with what I say and how I behave, or we could blow this thing right out of the water."

"Wonder what your 'mother' will have to say about that," Finn muttered under his breath.

Caeden looked out the window toward the setting sun. "Yes, well, I guess I'll deal with that when we get there. We leave for Oakhurst in the morning."

CHAPTER 19

They were being followed and had been for quite some time now, and Shea was finally certain of it. Though Connor seemed unaware, she still chose to keep it from him as he plodded forward over the rather treacherous terrain.

"You know, there is probably a place for you in my Mother's court," Connor told her, as he walked over the rocky slope. The rocks shifted precariously beneath his feet, and he took great care so as not to look foolish. A nasty spill would do that and hurt besides. "She is rather fond of you."

Shea chuckled at his misconception. "I find that rather difficult to believe," she said, concentrating on the task at hand while trying to remain cognizant of their surroundings. The pursuer was nowhere to be seen but that did not mean he was no longer there. If there was one thing her father taught her it was to always expect the unexpected. It would be the dog that would bite you in the ass if you didn't pay attention to it.

Clearing the rocks, they found themselves on a little higher elevation and Connor sat down for a moment. Refusing to sit, Shea surveyed the land below paying particular attention to the tree line they had just emerged from a short while ago. It ran along the base of the slope and provided perfect cover, especially if the being were familiar with the terrain.

"We need to keep going," Shea told Connor as she walked past him. "It will be dark soon."

Trying not to let out an audible groan, Connor rose from the rock he had perched on and started along after her. "Slave driver," he grumbled, half-joking yet half-serious.

"Shut up," she teased, "you'll thank me later.....Your *Highness*."

They continued onward until they reached an outcropping that provided a little shelter and a tactical advantage. From there they would be able to see anyone coming from three sides. Shea removed her traveling cloak and watched over Connor as he gathered up twigs for a fire. In the growing twilight she became a bit unnerved and was prepared to finally tell Connor they were being followed. At least then he would know and be able to help keep watch.

"Don't stray," she called out to him, taking care not to be too loud.

Connor shot her a look that told her he thought her a mother hen, and somewhat flustered she moved in his direction. Though older than she was, he sometimes acted like an overgrown child, and the last thing she had signed on for was a babysitting job.

"Yes, '*Mother*,'" he chided her, shaking his head. It had

been a long day's journey and it was beginning to take its toll on both of them at this point.

Shea stepped forward, mouth open ready to reply when it happened. Their pursuer, finally visible, dropped from the tree above Connor directly upon him taking him totally by surprise. Connor cried out in shock more than fear and set to defending himself. Though flat on his face on the ground, he managed to pull his legs up under him, reach his knees and push upward, rolling the assailant over.

Shea was at a full run over the short distance between her and Connor. Sword drawn, she shouted to Connor to get out of the way as she drew near. Still entangled with the other fae, he elbowed and wrestled around trying to free himself. Gaining just enough of an advantage, Connor managed to roll away as Shea pulled up short.

The assailant drew his sword and the moon's light flashed off the blade as it clashed with Shea's. She advanced swiftly and confidently, going into an instinctual mode that her father had taught her all those years ago as a child. From the moment he first put a sword in her hand, he had drilled and trained and instructed her that her duty first and foremost and, if done properly, last in life, would be that of protecting the royals.

Unarmed yet wanting to be of help, Connor searched the ground desperately for something to wield as a weapon. Finding a heavy tree branch he watched for the right moment to strike.

Shea didn't like being backed up one bit and shouted out as she fought harder, forcing the intruder to move back just a bit. The steel of the swords flashed in the moonlight as their blades sang out in a rhythm most familiar.

Unexpectedly, the assailant stopped.

Seeing her advantage, Shea took a run at him. He managed to get his sword in a defensive stance just in time, but it was too late. Wielding her blade, Shea ran it up along the length of his and looped it around, pulling hard to the side and sending it flying over near where Connor stood with his tree branch. With no other option at hand, the assailant did the only thing he could do. He raised his hands in defeat.

Not satisfied with his surrender, Shea turned about swiftly swinging her leg out and dropped her now-captive assailant flat on his back, knocking the wind out of him. He sucked in sharply, gasping for breath. She quickly slid her sword back in its sheath and sat with her full weight upon his chest, pinning his arms to the ground with her knees. She grabbed his wrists as she examined her dazed attacker.

Breathing hard, Shea tried to make out the face in the scant light. There was a familiarity to it, and she drew closer trying to identify him. Connor stepped up alongside her, picking the sword up off the ground. He examined it in the moonlight and recognized it instantly.

"I know this sword," Connor told her, though still pointing the weapon at the fae before them. "Forged in the fires of Ravensforge…"

"And blessed by the king himself," finished the breathless voice beneath her in the darkness. *"Hello, Shea."*

Chapter 20

In the moonlight Shea saw the face of a ghost from her recent past. Steel blue eyes stared up at her from the familiar chiseled face of one whom she had believed to have been yet another casualty of Ravensforge. Disbelief was mirrored back from his eyes to hers as her knees dug into the fleshy part of his upper arms keeping him securely pinned to the ground.

"Arn?" she asked, in shock as she examined the face. "Arn, is it really you?"

"Shea?" came back the familiar voice. *"Ow!* Yes! Yes, it's me. Now let me up!"

"Oh, sorry," she said, as she rose from his chest.

Connor observed it all from behind Shea, not quite certain what to think. He watched as Arn stood and brushed himself off. He was not much taller than Connor, and his arms and calves were well defined. His hair was shorn close to his head, creating nothing more than a shadow of stubble, really, and though he was muscular, he looked as though he'd been through a rough patch of late. His face was gaunt, and the pale moonlight only exaggerated the pallor of his skin.

Somewhat perplexed, she maintained a defensive stance. "Why were you following us?"

"No one has been through here in quite some time. I always follow along, hopeful it is someone I know, but it seems I am always wrong. When you came through here I immediately recognized the prince here from –" his words halted abruptly as he remembered their final night at Ravensforge, his capture and subsequent torture at the hands of the enemy.

Shea watched her dearest friend struggle with the memory. "Arn," she said softly, "I thought you were dead."

He looked down. "So did I."

Tentatively she lowered her sword and approached him. "I thought you were dead," she repeated, and leaned in to hug him, wrapping her free arm around his shoulders. Arn immediately relaxed and wrapped his arms around her. He drew back after a moment, holding her at arm's length so he could get a better look. In the moonlight, even with the shorter hair, she still looked like the friend he knew all those ages ago.

"I thought you'd been lost as well," he sighed, then smiled. "It is *so* good to see you."

Connor cleared his throat, feeling more like a third wheel than heir to the throne of Oakhurst. Jolted back into the present, Shea withdrew from Arn's embrace and looked at Connor.

"Arn, may I present Connor, Crown Prince of Oakhurst," she said. "Connor, this is my best friend, Arn."

The pair sized each other up, and even in the dim light

following the fight he'd just witnessed, he judged Arn to be quite fit and strong in spite of his gaunt face and hollowed out cheeks. He would make a good traveling companion. If, that is, he could be trusted.

It was one thing for Shea to trust him but a totally different thing for Connor. If there was one thing his father had taught him, it was to be careful with whom one made his allegiances. Connor himself had learned that even if one had known a fae for most of his life, they still could not be trusted completely. Power corrupts, and it did not matter whether young and naïve or old and seemingly wise, the possibility was always there.

"Majesty," Arn said, minding his place and bowing low, "it is an honor to make your acquaintance."

Connor nodded slightly, glancing over at Shea and looking very awkward. He was less on formality and more on the adventurous side of royalty. His mother was none too happy about that. Besides, it was his lust for adventure that had gotten him into this mess in the first place.

"The pleasure is mine, Arn of Ravensforge," Connor said.

ᛒᚩ   ᚳᚷ

The trio gathered wood and managed to build a decent fire near the cliff face. Shea watched Arn as the firelight danced on his face. It warmed her heart to see him again. It was as if a family member was back from the dead. Poking the embers with a stick, she finally spoke.

"How long have you been out here?"

Arn sighed. "Not as long as one would think," he answered slowly, drawing in a deep breath. "I spent a great deal of time in the dungeon of Erebos."

157

"No longer merely a legend."

"If it is only legend, then legend must be redefined." He looked down at the fire, grappling with the memory, sifting through it in an attempt to determine what to share and what to leave out.

"After the royals made it to the portal, I thought you would have a better chance if I bought you more time. Once I saw they made it through, I tried to make a run for it." His brows knit together as the painful memories washed over him. "They were everywhere – coming out of the sky and up from the ground, swallowing me up like some massive blackness with a thousand arms and claws and nasty green eyes."

"Gutiku," Shea said quietly, remembering her own experience with the nasty creatures. They had been small in the human realm, but in the fae realm, in the form they were in now, the Gutiku were even bigger than they were. And that frightened Shea. "How did you get away?"

Arn swallowed hard. "They hauled me back to Erebos and locked me away for days without food or water. I thought I would perish, and that would have been preferable to being ripped limb from limb by their claws. I prayed I would just go to sleep and never wake up."

The firelight danced on their faces as Arn began his tale. The chill that ran down Shea's spine had little to do with the breeze that blew in off the water nearby. They were close to the Castle Erebos – she could feel it, and it scared her.

"The legends are not at all accurate," Arn said, as he stirred the fire with a stick. "The tales your father would tell us as children? Do you remember how frightened you would be, Shea?" he laughed softly at the memory. "That is nothing compared to the evil within the walls of Erebos."

158

Arn's eyes were vacant as he talked, and Shea could see the pain behind them. If it weren't absolutely crucial that he relate the information to them, she would have changed the subject then and there. But there was too much at stake this time. Too much for them to lose, and she knew that she was the one who had to retrieve the Keeper of Time. And if The Dark Warrior of Erebos was the one who had been behind the theft, she was the one who would have to face him.

"Arn, I'm so sorry," was all she could manage.

They sat in silence for a short time, processing all that Arn had said.

"So what has become of Beltran's daughters?" Arn asked Shea finally, taking his eyes from the flames for only a moment. Shea didn't know what to make of it. He was so distant. It was as if the flames between them were as big as the fires of hell, and his presence a few feet from her may have well been half a realm away.

"I do not know," Shea answered. "When they went through the portal, they went to wherever we were supposed to end up. As the Messenger approached and struck the portal with the staff's energy, the flow from our realm to the human realm jumped to a different place." She looked at Connor. "Oakhurst."

"And I see you now bear that same staff," Arn noted.

"Yes, well," Shea replied, "it took some doing to get it."

Connor sat across from her and she could sense something was off with him, but she couldn't quite put her finger on it. He had been acting strangely since Arn's arrival, but it was more than that. His movements were slower, as if he were pained when he walked. Connor also seemed to have trouble tracking their conversation. He looked from Arn's face to hers

159

but said nothing.

"Connor, are you alright?" she asked.

A moment passed before he spoke. "Yes," he said rather unconvincingly, "yes, I am fine. I am merely tired, that's all. Arn, please continue."

"When he sent us out, Guntram said that the portal would reach the Kingdom of Oakhurst," Arn told them. "It would appear that you ended up in the right place, and it is the princesses who went elsewhere."

"Interesting," Connor noted.

"Well, that would make sense," Shea answered. "Think about it. Why go to the human realm and be completely away from all you know, everyone you know? Yes, there is the size difference, but still they are there."

"It would have been possible to offer them counsel even if they were in human form."

"This is true," Connor said, remembering his own experience. "It would also be easy to settle old scores with one's enemies."

"That would explain the Messenger's presence at Minnetrista. Darius Pendragon was unknown to me because I did not remember him. I did not remember what happened that night," Shea's voice was filled with regret at being able to do nothing to help Arn, "what he'd done to you."

She looked at Arn for a long moment. His eyes were still focused on the flames. He offered her only a glance up, and in that brief second as their eyes met, she knew the pain in his remembering that night. It seared in his eyes. He recognized instantly that she knew and went immediately back to tending the fire.

"We should get some rest," Arn said, changing the subject.

Shea knew he was done with it and did not press him further. "I'll take first watch," she said.

Both young men protested, more out of chivalry than desire to keep watch, but they knew it was useless to argue with her. They also knew how capable she was, and that they were safe in her hands. They settled in for the night.

"Wake me if you need anything," Connor said, as he laid back and closed his eyes.

"There is little between here and Erebos," Shea answered with a slight smile, "and we're still too far out for anyone there to take notice of us."

"Let's hope that you are right."

CHAPTER 21

Verena sat by the fire as the pixie brought her a warm drink to take the chill off. It felt good, but she knew she didn't have much time to waste. The pixie climbed up on a stepstool, then rummaged around for a time through several boxes before she found what she was looking for.

Settling in next to the fire, she looked up at Verena.

"I saw the humans breaking the ice on the river early yesterday morning. There was much sadness among them. Did they know your brother?"

Verena sighed. "No, not really. They had an idea of who he was as a human, but beyond that they knew nothing more than the fact that he was a man who had a most unfortunate accident."

"Tell me, Princess," the pixie said in a more civil tone, "what happened to my friend, Royce?"

"He sacrificed himself to stop the Gutiku from destroying my kingdom as well as his own."

The pixie smiled sadly. "Yes, that sounds like my Royce."

Verena shifted at the pixie's familiarity with Royce, but sensed that it was nothing more than a deep and abiding friendship between them.

"Connor used one of Elisabeth's magic boxes to entrap the Gutiku, but Royce was pulled in with them."

The pixie was silent as she considered the loss of her friend.

"Those on the outskirts of Nebosham, they told me that you and Royce were close," Verena said. "King Rogan treated you poorly?"

"King Rogan is a fool," the little one replied, "and he's not very nice either."

Verena chuckled at her frankness. "I am afraid I have to agree with you on that count," she said.

"When he discovered our friendship, he banished me from the gardens surrounding Nebosham. *Psssshhhht!* Like he can really do that."

"And yet you are here instead of in the gardens," Verena pointed out.

"I've moved up in the world."

"Pixie, what is your name?"

"I am called Niwadi," the pixie replied, "and I bear no grudge against you, Princess. It is Rogan who believes the pixies are no better than the dirt beneath his feet. Kind of like how the fae look upon the sprites."

"Not all fae look upon them that way," Verena said. "There are those –"

"—like you."

"—like me, who look upon them as equals. Unfortunately, King Rogan is willing to go to war over something that we should instead be working together to solve. He still grieves for his son, and he is channeling his anger in this way."

"So you seek those who are dead?"

Sadness clouded Verena's eyes as she spoke. "I am not convinced that they are dead."

"Is that your logic talking or your grief?"

"I wish I knew."

ೞ   ೦೪

Caeden sat alone in the darkness of his princely quarters. He stared out the window toward the west contemplating how he would ever set this mess straight.

The queen would have his head for sure over this one. She had shown him mercy at the urging of Arland and later Connor, but this situation could throw them into war with Hawksgate. Their isolation and mastery of the hawks gave them the upper hand militarily. But he knew that misperceptions on the part of King Astor and his advisors had simply gotten out of hand. One thing was for sure: there was no turning back now.

He pondered the implications of their mission as they stood when they left Oakhurst. *Find the portal, nothing more, then return and report.* Those had been their instructions. Obviously, things had gotten out of hand. And improvisation, though seemingly successful thus far, was not Caeden's strong suit. He only hoped he would fare as well before Queen Liliana, if only in the act of pleading his case.

It could, in fact, be his last.

165

CHAPTER 22

Connor could feel it. Something just didn't sit right with Arn's story. He didn't know the fae...didn't care much about him. But Connor had gotten to know Shea, had begun to truly care about her. He wasn't about to see her hurt.

Unfortunately, she could see nothing but her oldest friend back from the dead, and for Shea, this was nothing more than cause for celebration. Connor saw it as cause for caution. This was no time to get sentimental. The stakes were too high and time was growing short to reach their objective.

Getting a moment alone with her, he finally spoke up about his misgivings.

"Great having your friend back, huh?" he asked rather awkwardly.

"Of course," Shea replied.

Arn was several steps ahead as they walked along through

167

the meadow. Shea took care to watch their surroundings and remained mindful of Connor as he walked beside her.

"So you know him well?" Connor asked of her without looking her way.

"Yes," Shea answered back. "We grew up together. His father was my father's best friend." Shea was watching the back of Arn's head. She glanced over to find Connor watching her. "When his father was lost in battle, my father took him in. He's as close as family to me."

"I see," Connor responded, looking down to just in front of him. He sensed that it was more than that for Arn, but didn't want to tell her that, didn't want to discuss it at all unless she was already aware of it. They plodded along in silence before Shea spoke again.

"I trust him with my life," Shea answered the question that hung unspoken between them. "He grew up the same as I did, learned the same things as I did," she paused, "has the same commitment to duty and honor as I do."

Connor looked at her, not sure of what to say. He decided to remain silent on the matter, turning instead back to watching Arn.

"Connor," Shea said, stopping. Connor stopped a few feet ahead of her and turned around. "I trust him with my life," she repeated. "And yours."

"Let us pray you are right in your assessment."

"Just what exactly are you getting at?" she asked rather pointedly. "I thought we'd gone over this already."

"Simply that caution might best serve us out here," he said, choosing his words carefully. The last thing he wanted to do was alienate her.

Connor watched as Shea paused for a moment considering

168

his words. He had not steered her wrong yet, nor she him, and they had been through a lot together. If there was one thing he knew, it was that he trusted Shea with his life. And he believed *that trust* ran both ways.

But for as much as she believed she could trust Arn, Connor found he could not. At least not yet. He would take some convincing, and Shea would have to be the one to convince him before it all came crashing down around them.

"Agreed," Shea replied, much to Connor's amazement, and it registered on his face. "You seem surprised."

"No, no," Connor backpedaled, trying to cover his tracks. She knew him too well for him to lie to her over something like this, and he knew he was caught. "Well, perhaps I am a little concerned."

She shot him a look that told him he'd gone in the wrong direction. "Arn can be trusted. You'll see."

"Does he know about the amulet?" Connor asked point blank.

Shea looked around. Arn was nowhere to be found. "What?"

"When Beltran gave you the amulet, was Arn there? Does he know you have it?"

"No," she said slowly, not liking where this was going.

"Let's keep it that way," Connor said, watching something that looked like anger rising in Shea. "Just until we know he can be trusted."

"I know he can be," Shea replied rather curtly.

"Well, he'll have to earn my trust," Connor said, "and it would appear, Shea of Ravensforge, that I outrank you."

ഇ   ൫

It had been a day of turmoil in the palace of Oakhurst. Queen Liliana was utterly beside herself. Already distraught at the loss of her son, then to find her daughter missing was almost more than the monarch could bear.

Though the queen had yet to say it, Rayne knew it was her fault. She also knew it would most likely end her service career as well. She had heard tales through the ranks of Caeden's mishandling of the prince's protection and had even agreed with the course of action Queen Liliana had taken in dismissing him. But now that the shoe was on the other foot, Rayne knew firsthand of the difficulties involved in protecting a royal that did not wish to be protected.

The Royal Guard had been in and around Oakhurst Gardens throughout the day, and their search had been exhaustive. The cold weather didn't help at all, and the blowing snow only served to cover any possible way to track Verena should she be on the ground. Most likely, she had taken to flight, in which case they would never be able to track her.

It was Arland who kept the queen apprised of their progress even when there was little of nothing to report. That had been the case most of the day, and though Arland had recalled them, many continued to search.

As the sun set, Rayne vowed to look on. After all, what else was there for her to do?

One thing was for certain: there was nothing left for her at the palace if she did not find Princess Verrena.

ᛒᚩ   ᚳᚷ

It was well past nightfall when Verena and Niwadi

170

returned to the secret garden behind the L.L. Ball house further down Minnetrista Boulevard just outside the gates of Oakhurst. Knowing that her mother would have guards searching for her, she had relocated the magic box to a new hiding place before setting out in search of the pixie.

The snow was cold and deep, and Verena chose to walk instead of fly so Niwadi would not think her rude. The last thing she could afford to do was alienate the only being who could help her. Both were dressed for the weather, but it was harsh nonetheless.

Niwadi took the knapsack from her shoulder and tossed it on top of the snow. It sunk slightly, but the magic she'd packed with her was light, and the tools were such as well. She dug through the bag, shoulder deep at times, before finding exactly what she was searching for.

"Princess, trade me cloaks," she said, handing Verena the black cloth from her bag.

Without question Verena shed her royal traveling cloak and handed it to Niwadi in exchange for the garment she offered. She wrapped it around her, pulled the hood up and tied it at the neck. It was lightweight, almost as if it weren't there, but surprisingly warm.

"You will be moving in the realm of dark magic," Niwadi told her. "It is a strange place. Not really a realm at all. More accurately, one might say it is located somewhere between the realms of fae and humans. This cloak will allow you to move about freely while you are there."

"How will I find Royce? And Connor and Shea – what about them? Will I find them there as well?"

"If Royce still lives, you will find him there. As for your brother and friend, I cannot say." Niwadi looked around her at the snow-covered ground. "Now, where did you put the magic box?"

Verena led her to a faerie statue that the humans had placed in the garden. Behind it, Verena began to clear the snow away to reveal a dry, withered patch of groundcover. She pulled at the sinewy remains of the plants to uncover the box that was still tied up securely in the ribbon Royce had handed off to her.

"Verena, remember: I must tie the lid on once you are inside. And whatever you do, don't lose the cape. You will only be able to return from the box wearing the cape. Any who are covered with it will also escape."

Verena looked down at the cape. It was barely big enough to wrap around herself, let alone anyone else. Puzzled, she looked at Niwadi unsure of what to say.

Rolling her eyes the pixie tromped through the snow, took hold of the corner of the cape and held it high to demonstrate. Grinning up at Verena, she twirled herself in toward the princess, showing her instantly that the cape was more than enough to wrap them both in with room to spare.

"It'll grow with you," Niwadi teased. "Trust me."

"Niwadi, thank you," Verena said warmly.

"Don't thank me yet," the pixie said. "Two minutes on the other side of that lid and you'll be cursing me, I guarantee it."

Verena's eyes widened.

"Then you'd better send me quick before I lose my nerve."

CHAPTER 23

Niwadi looked at Verena and slowly pulled the ribbon on the magic box. Handmade by Elisabeth herself, it was weathered and worn but still solid in construction. She put her full weight on the lid as she untied the last of the knot.

"Remember," the pixie told her, "don't lose the cape."

"Got it," Verena said, looking back at her nervously. "Just in case, what happens if I lose it?"

"You'll be on holiday in that bloody-awful box for a very long time."

Verena smiled nervously. "I won't lose the cape."

"Ready?"

"Ready."

Niwadi slid off the top of the box and lifted the lid just enough so that Verena could climb in. It would have been much easier had her wings been exposed, but the cape was obviously a necessity that could not even be remotely placed in jeopardy.

Once Verena was inside, Niwadi slammed the lid shut behind her. In the darkness she could hear the ribbon being slid back up across the lid and tied back securely.

"It's dark in here!" Verena hissed to Niwadi, as she sat upon the lid.

"*Pshhht!* Silly princess, check the pockets," the pixie chided her. "Do you think I would send you in search of my best friend in the dark? Your victory will be mine as well."

Verena's anxiety level began to rise as she fumbled through the pockets. "Well, if it's so important, why aren't you in here with me?"

"Somebody had to tie the lid shut."

€   &#x3;

Shea had noticed for days now but hesitated to say anything, partly out of paranoia but mostly out of the sheer fact that she knew something was wrong. And the longer she trudged along the pathway, the more she knew she was right.

The Dragon's Staff was hexed!

There could be no other possible explanation.

Ever since their return to the faerie realm, she had noticed it weighed more and more with each passing day. By her measure they had been there for nearly a week, and at first she just passed it off as merely exhaustion from their rather unorthodox arrival. Being sucked under the icy surface of the White River while in pursuit of the one-eyed troll would stress even the heartiest of souls. She was convinced that the troll held the answers to the whereabouts of the Keeper of Time.

She was certain that the Dark Warrior already knew where they were and that they were coming for the relic. And she believed with all her heart that he wasn't scared a bit.

Her arms ached as she shifted it from one hand to the other. Connor was three steps in front of her and hadn't noticed, but Arn had. He was just off her right shoulder only half a step behind and had never been one to miss much.

"You seem to grow weary," he noted, as they walked along.

"It's nothing," Shea told him. She dared not look at him because out of everyone she knew, he was most able to read her eyes, to see straight through to her heart. One did not spend as much time with another as they had growing up and miss things like that. "Ours was an arduous arrival here, and I am simply…tired," she said.

"They say the weight of a responsibility such as this is great upon the one who bears it."

Shea stopped in her tracks and stared after Arn. He was a few steps beyond her when he turned to look at her. It was as if he had read her mind.

"How long have you known?"

"Awhile," Arn answered quietly. "It is still not abundantly apparent but soon will be."

"I cannot give it up." Shea told him. "It is my burden. Mine alone."

"Understood. Just know that you are not alone in this fight. You are my family – the only family I have left – and I will protect you with my life."

"And I you." she said automatically, as she always did, but the words rang hollow to her at the thought of all Arn had suffered at the hands of the Gutiku and the Dark Warrior. Her guilt flashed across her face before she could conceal it, and she could tell from the look in his eyes that Arn had seen it.

"Shea, it wasn't your fault."

"If only I –"

"Your first responsibility, then and now, is to the royals. The Princesses of Ravensforge, the Prince of Oakhurst, it makes no difference. Your first duty is to protect them. You will honor that vow just as I will. There is no shame in that."

"Agreed. But my path has changed slightly. I have become something more than I was before. Something that has changed the way I look at things. Not in a big way, it's just different. I now protect them all: Oakhurst, Nebosham, Hawksgate. I am responsible for protecting all of them, royal and common alike."

"You have my assistance for as long as you want it."

"Thank you, my friend. I am glad to have found you again."

"As am I."

ೞ   ೞ

At the far end of the garden Rayne discovered two tiny sets of tracks in the snow. Afraid to hope, she followed them anyway in spite of the fact it might be nothing more than pesky sprites. And she surmised they would be of little help.

It was then that she spied a pixie making her way toward the east boundary of the property. She was moving fairly quickly, and Rayne needed to rush just to catch up.

"Pixie," Rayne addressed her when she'd managed to catch up, "what is your business here?"

The pixie kept walking. Rubbing her hands together to

warm them, she moved with determination to get in out of the cold. Frustrated by her lack of response, Rayne took flight, landing directly in the pixie's path.

"What do you want?" Niwadi demanded of the guard.

"Please, I only wish to know if you have seen Princess Verena of Oakhurst this day."

The pixie's eyes narrowed. "Why do you seek her?"

"Please," Rayne pleaded, "I am her guard, sworn to protect her at all costs. Her mother is beside herself, sick with worry. I wish only to ease her mind with the safe return of her daughter."

"And save your own neck as well, I'd wager," Niwadi shot back, her voice taking an edge to it.

"My fate is of little consequence at this point. I only know that the kingdom cannot suffer another blow such as this. It would be devastating," Rayne told her.

"Where she has gone you cannot follow," Niwadi said, as she began to walk again.

"Wait! What?" Rayne stammered, moving to catch up. "You know where she is? Where she has gone?"

"Perhaps."

"Tell me! I must go to her at once!"

Niwadi stopped walking, turned to the guard and sighed. "You cannot go where Verena has gone."

Frustrated, Rayne was ready to draw her sword and drag the pixie back to the palace by her fiery red hair. "Why can I not follow her?"

"Because I only have one cloak, and she has it."

છ   ૭

Shea's stomach growled as it gnawed voraciously at her backbone. It had been more than a day since they'd eaten anything of substance, and she could feel herself growing weaker by the hour. Connor was putting on a brave front, but she'd known him long enough to sense his true state of being.

"Let us rest here," she said quietly, as she came upon a group of rocks. She rested the Dragon Staff against the boulder and surveyed their surroundings.

Connor said nothing as he leaned up against a boulder and slowly lowered himself onto an adjacent rock. He rested his head against the taller of the two and closed his eyes.

"He grows weak," Arn observed. His lips were dry and cracked for want of water. He wiped the sweat from his brow with his sleeve as he looked up to the sky. The sun was barely past mid-day, and they both knew it was too soon to stop.

"We'll rest here awhile," Shea echoed herself, "then press on until just before dark. How much further do you think?"

"Another day's walk at best. But with Connor beginning to fail, it will most likely take longer."

Drawing in a deep breath, Shea sighed. Her brows knit together, and for a moment she thought she might be losing her mind.

"What is it?" Arn asked. He knew that look.

Shea inhaled deeply again. "Do you smell that?" She smiled, exhaled, then drew in another deep breath.

Frowning, Arn followed suit, doing the same. Confusion crossed his face as he exhaled, then sucked in a deep breath, his chest filled to capacity.

"Food," Connor said quietly. "Someone's cooking food."

CHAPTER 24

Arn helped Connor to his feet as Shea took off in the direction of the delicious aroma that had so enticed her nostrils. She couldn't quite put her finger on what it was – and didn't really care for that matter – but it reminded her of some of Jackie's fabulous fare at the diner.

She had wandered into a stand of trees. Hearing Arn and Connor following behind her through the weeds, she made her way along. Her feet got tangled several times, and she steadied herself with the staff. She was already weakened and could only imagine how much worse Connor felt.

Shea stopped at her destination and smiled. "I found it!" she called to the others.

Before her was a dark hole in the stone outcropping. Covered in a tangle of dead vines, it looked imposing, yet the aroma floating out on the cool breeze was so inviting.

"Hello?" Shea called into the cave, as Connor and Arn

came up behind her. "Is anybody there?"

"I do not think that wise," Arn observed. "It could be anybody."

"Right now I don't care if it's the Dark Warrior of Erebos so long as he's fixing us sausage gravy and biscuits," she muttered.

"It's official," Connor chimed it, "she's lost it."

"I'll go in," Arn told them, passing Connor off to Shea to support. Shea began to protest but knew better of it.

Arn stepped up to the tangle of vines covering the opening of the cave, carefully weighing his options. He looked over his shoulder at them, then turning back he raised a hand to move the vines. A sharp *CRACK!* greeted his hand, and he quickly withdrew it. Electrical in nature, it made the hair on his arms and the back of his neck stand on end.

Shea and Connor moved over to the cave. "Maybe you won't," she said.

"Let me try," Connor said. He tottered a moment, steadied himself, moving the few steps toward the tangle. He paused, raising a hand and eased his palm ever closer to the mouth of the cave. It sizzled and cracked as his hand approached like the downed power lines a short time ago back in Muncie.

The aroma continued to waft out, growing stronger and changing slightly. There was a sweetness to it reminding Shea of a dish her father used to prepare when she was a child. Unable to bear it anymore, staff in hand, she stepped up and walked right into the tangle of vines. No sizzle, no crackle, only the smells of food being prepared over an open fire. She turned and looked back at her stunned traveling companions.

She smiled at them knowing in her gut that it could very well be a trap.

180

"I won't be long," she told them, "and I promise, I won't eat it all."

↊   ↋

Shea moved slowly into the darkness of the cave. The mouth of the cavern was overgrown with vines and foliage, and she moved them out of her path as she made her way in amongst them. It was a rather claustrophobic feeling, really, and she was starting to feel something akin to panic begin to rise up in her as she went deeper into the dark tangle of vines.

The staff got caught twice, and she weighed the value of taking it further but couldn't fathom leaving it behind for fear she might need it.

The growing blackness was disquieting and after a moment's pause, she reached up to the chain around her neck and pulled the amulet up out of her tunic. With nothing between it and the staff, both began to glow brighter. Though it wasn't much, it afforded her just enough light to see what was directly in front of her, which were more vines.

At one point she thought about turning back, but she'd gone just far enough that she wasn't certain she knew exactly which direction she'd come from. On more than one occasion she found her arms tangled in the foliage and was ready to take out her sword to use it as a machete when she finally reached the other side. Just ahead in the darkness she could see torchlight.

She paused, feeling a cool breeze upon her face. It was an updraft, and she was just about to take a step forward when something flew up out of the floor in front of her. She flung herself backward and found herself lying in a startled heap on

181

the floor of the cavern amongst the vines. The staff clattered to rest on the stone floor next to her.

She found that the amulet and staff gave her more light closer to the ground for some reason, so she crawled across the cool, damp floor making her way back to where she'd been. Her stomach cartwheeled when she saw where she'd stood only moments before.

There was a huge drop-off directly in front of her. She couldn't see more than a few feet away, but the breeze coming up out of the pit was enough to tell her that it was a long, long way down. Looking back up at the torch that was on the wall no more than fifteen feet away, she kept close to the ground minding the edge of the pit. She crawled to the right, edging along the hole until she reached the end of it. Three feet later she found the wall.

She crawled slowly, ever so cautiously along. At one point her hand slid off the edge, sending rocks and debris cascading down into the abyss. Her other arm caught her weight shift just in time to keep her from plummeting downward. Taking a deep, shuddering breath Shea leaned against the cold wall briefly to regain her composure. Finally she moved on.

Even though she thought she was clear of the other side of the pit, she remained on all fours, making her way toward the torch. The goal was to keep from being surprised, and the amulet provided just enough light to get the job done.

Reaching her goal, Shea slid her shoulder up the wall, steadying herself with the staff until she stood at eye-level with the bracket that held the torch to the wall. She reached up and took it from its place. Though it afforded precious little more light than the relics had, it was a source of comfort more than anything.

The blackness surrounded Shea enveloping her as it separated her from the rest of the realm, and she felt a rising apprehension with each step she took. Her boots brought a slight echo back from the walls, and an occasional breeze made her stop to reassess her choices. After the first pit, she was mindful of the floor, gingerly choosing her steps as she went.

The five foot radius around her from the torchlight seemed small in the black cavern. She held it out at arm's length in front of her to give her a little extra light and was nearly ready to turn back when something in the distance caught her eye.

Shea decided to use the staff as a feeler before her, and she grasped it just beneath the headpiece. It gave her an extra few feet beyond the light and a sense of security, if only in knowing what lie immediately before her.

The smell of food was growing stronger now, and Shea was determined to find it. Stomach protesting even louder now, she followed her nose.

Suddenly a sound a short distance behind Shea startled her, and she dropped the staff. Glad to have the torch, she quickly recovered it and picked up her pace. She was well aware that Connor and Arn could not enter the cave, so at this point it seemed prudent to press on than attempt to deal with whatever might be behind her.

Thoughts of the Gutiku and their horrible visits to Ravensforge and Oakhurst sent a chill down her spine. She swiftly set aside the memories of how they had come up from the ground and attacked Arn and how they had dragged poor Royce into the magic box with them.

Torch in her left hand and the staff wedged tightly under the same arm, she reached across her body and withdrew the sword from her sheath with her right. The firelight danced along the blade as she raised it to the ready. Her gear weighed her down and her stance was awkward at best. Truth be told, if anything came at her in the dark, what with the load she was hauling, it would be all over in a matter of moments.

It was a small light which played tricks on her eyes in the darkness at first. It appeared no larger than a firefly would to a human, and Shea surmised it was merely a long way down the corridor. Lowering the torch slightly to keep her eye on the floor in front of her while she advanced her position, she crept silently along. On more than one occasion she paused, feeling a draft to her left or right. Moving the torch in either direction, she saw nothing beyond the small circle of light and decided that whatever lay beyond the illumination was best left unseen.

After what felt like hours of plodding along, the light ahead of her grew larger in size until she could make out a lit entryway. Sword at the ready, she moved to the cavern wall in an attempt to conceal herself somewhat, although the torch in her hand wouldn't do her much good in that respect. Ever so carefully she peered around the corner of the doorway.

The small room was well-lit with torches all around and a large, warm fire burning in the center of the room. There were provisions along the back wall, and a pot hung on a tripod over the fire with rather delicious smelling contents bubbling away.

Shea's stomach growled in response to the smell, and she pulled back from the doorway. After a moment's silence she peered around the corner again, and seeing no one, she returned the sword to its sheath and stepped into the well-lit room.

She leaned the staff against the wall and made her way around along the wall looking at all that was there. Makeshift shelves had been carved into the cave walls and were lined with a variety of jars, bottles and sundry other trinkets. There were dusty boxes, similar to those Elisabeth had made and left in the gardens of Oakhurst for Queen Liliana and King Rogan, and in the corner rested a hawk's feather as tall as she was.

Slowly, she stepped past the feather. It was several shades of tan with beautiful brown markings, and the down at the top of the quill looked soft in spite of the dust that covered the remainder of the feather. She reached up to touch it, her fingers just short of caressing the down when she heard a boot scuff the floor behind her. She wheeled on her heels, in one fluid motion dropping the torch as she drew her sword. When she stopped one hundred and eighty degrees later, she stood at the ready, prepared for battle. What she discovered next shocked her to the core.

Standing before her, dressed in ragged yet distinctly royal clothing, was a man. Rather unkempt and unshaven, he merely looked at the intruder and smiled.

"Well," he said with a rich, deep voice, "it's about bloody time."

❧   ☙

The small blue orb in the palm of her hand glowed as Verena made her way into the expanse of the box. She was surprised at how big it was on the inside, noting that for a place that was said to be between realms, it was incredibly spacious. She could hear her own footsteps echoing as she walked along as if she were the only one in a vast chamber.

Verena sensed that there were others there with her but did not feel threatened. It was unnerving, to say the least, and unfortunately the orb offered precious little light to guide her way.

Verena was not sure if her eyes were merely adjusting to the darkness, or if there were finally a source of light coming from somewhere. On one wall was what appeared to be a window. It cast a faint pallor into the room and she stepped nearer to it.

Had she been one to give in to panic, she would have been cursing Niwadi just as the pixie had predicted, were it not for the fact that she was desperate. *Incredibly desperate.*

Stepping up to the window, she was relieved to see the sky. But it was not as it should be. And she recognized the surrounding landscape and buildings. It was the koi pond behind the L.L. Ball house, and Verena found she was looking skyward through it!

The stars above Oakhurst Gardens were beautiful and brighter than Verena ever remembered. The moon, though waning with only a sliver missing, shone magnificently on all below it. The princess found it breathtaking in spite of the fact she was scared half out of her wits.

Taking care not to linger, she turned and made her way on into the cavernous space. Still too soon to know if it were a room or a palace or some hellish sort of place that defied description, she found a strange comfort in the darkness. It was almost as if she were a child again playing the game her father taught her to increase her intuitive skills.

"Trust your instincts, Verena," she recalled the king saying, as he walked around behind her. "They will serve you well."

In her mind's eye Verena stood in the middle of the throne room of Oakhurst, eyes closed. They were alone, as it was each day, and he would teach her how to use her gift of discernment. She had discovered at a very early age that she knew when fae were lying or being deceitful. It was as if she could peer into their very souls and see if they were of light or darkness, whether their hearts were of good character, the product of lousy upbringing, or somewhere in between.

"Yes, Father," she replied.

Taking the feather of a hawk from a tall vase next to his throne – a gift from the king of Hawksgate – he moved toward his daughter. The feather was nearly as tall as he but was easy to wield, and they'd played this game since she was very small.

"Your senses will only stand in your way," King Marco told her. "Though it is only a feather I wield, it may as well be a sword. Let your instinct guide you always. Trust it and you will never fail."

"Yes, Father," she said again.

"At the ready!" he called from directly behind her.

Verena took a deep breath and exhaled slowly as she began listening with her entire body. The temperature variations around her, the subtle movements of the air, she drank it all in.

"Ready, Father."

Swiftly, he had already moved around to her left side taking a swing at her head with the tail feather. Verena's arm flew into a defensive position with lightning reflexes blocking it well before it reached its intended mark.

Again, the feather came over her head, aiming for the right side of her neck. In a flash the arm on the other side of her body flew up, crooked at the elbow effectively blocking it from striking her neck.

Over and over, her father drilled her on making use of her gifts in hopes of one day making her his most trusted advisor. But he knew that would have to wait until she was older. Merely an adolescent at the time, she still had much to learn. King Marco could only hope that there would be enough time to teach it all to her.

Unfortunately for Verena, time had run out for her father, and he was ripped from her life. She smiled at the memory of him but still missed him greatly after all this time.

She often thought that if he were truly not gone, she would know. But to this day, she felt no presence of him within the realm and had made her peace with that fact long ago.

Verena half-wished she had a weapon with her but knew it would do her little good in this place. It was filled with the nasty Gutiku that had claimed her Royce, but for some reason they were dormant. She sensed nothing of them and decided she would not concern herself with them until she felt the need to.

She walked slowly past a series of windows. Through one she could see up into the underside of the bridge that Niwadi lived in. The White River shimmered above her in the pre-dawn light. The sun would be up soon, and though she did not feel a need for expediency, she preferred to remain in this place no longer than absolutely necessary.

The further inward she went, the less familiar she became with the water windows as she passed them by. Some were no bigger than mud puddles. Others were lakes. Still some beyond that were vast, shimmering panes that seemed to continue on forever, and she welcomed the oncoming light as

188

it began to fill the cavernous room.

She felt as if she were traveling farther and faster than one would expect to, almost as if the waters were side by side instead of at a distance from one another. Verena knew this was not the case and was hopeful that it might speed up her search.

She could just make out shadowy figures in the distance and knew that the coming daylight would reveal more – much more – than she cared to see.

That, she decided, *would not be good at all.*

CHAPTER 25

Shea sat in front of the roaring fire, plate of stew in hand. She gobbled the hot food down as if she hadn't eaten in weeks. Though it felt that way, they had only gone a couple of days subsisting on what little edible vegetation they had managed to scrounge along the way.

The man watched her finish the stew, then reached for the pot to get her more. Still chewing, Shea held her hand up, and he stopped in mid reach. "Are you sure?" he asked. "There's plenty more."

Shea shook her head and finished chewing. "No, thank you," she said finally. "It was delicious and most appreciated."

The man took the empty plate from her and placed it on the table on the opposite side of the chamber. He was at least a full head taller than Shea, and though rather gaunt in appearance, he carried himself with strength and authority. She watched as he walked back toward her and took a seat just a few feet away.

"You are Guard, are you not?" he inquired, noting her armor.

Shea nodded, careful not to reveal too much. She was still uncertain who she was dealing with and felt the need to err on the side of caution with her words.

"I do not know you," she said rather pointedly. "You appear to be of royal lineage, and while I am acquainted with the royals of three of the four kingdoms, I do not recognize you."

"You probably wouldn't," he said with a slight, hollow laugh. "I have been gone a very long time. My own family probably wouldn't even recognize me at this point." Sadness veiled his face and he sighed heavily.

Shea watched as he poked the fire with a stick in an attempt to regain his composure. Giving him an out, she attempted to change the subject. "How long have you been here, in this place?"

"Too long to measure," he responded. "I am not certain, actually. All I know is that my family has surely moved on, and my children are probably grown by now."

The fire was warm and silence hung in the air between them for a few moments. Finally, it was Shea who spoke up.

"I am Shea of Ravensforge," she told the man, "Guardian of the Royal Daughters of King Beltran and Queen Astra."

"Oh, *now* we're getting somewhere," the man said, his deep voice resonating throughout the room as he straightened. "How is Beltran? Still as arrogant as ever, I suppose."

His frankness and slight disrespect for her king angered her somewhat, and she pushed it back down before her words got her into trouble.

192

"The king," Shea said, measuring her words and their tone carefully, "is missing."

"Missing?"

"Ravensforge was destroyed on the heels of a state dinner held in honor of the introduction of the King's daughters to Connor, Crown Prince of Oakhurst," she informed him. "One of them was to be betrothed to him in marriage."

"Marriage?" the man asked, the surprise apparent on his face. "Why, he's not ready for marriage. Connor's merely a boy!"

Shea was caught off guard by the man's knowledge of Connor. "You know him?"

The man's deep laughter echoed in the chamber, and he nearly fell off of his seat. "Know him? *Know* him?! Well, that's rich..."

She waited and watched until he was finished with his outburst. *His mind must be going*, she surmised silently. *He has apparently spent way too much time alone in this place.*

"Know him?" the man asked again as the laughter subsided, tears running down his cheek. "Of course, I *know* him....I'm his father."

CHAPTER 26

"You are the King of Oakhurst? *King Marco?"* Shea asked in surprise. Caught off guard, yet knowing her place, she knelt before him and bowed her head. "Your Majesty."

"Get up, child," he said, placing a hand on her shoulder. "If I had wanted this kind of reception, I would have announced myself an hour ago."

Shea returned to her seat and studied his face for a moment. Though dirty and unshaven, the face was familiar to her, yet his eyes did resemble Connor's. "How long have you been here?" she asked. "How did you get here?"

"Too long to measure," he said with a sigh. "And how I got here, well, let's just say it's a long story."

Shea smiled. "You look like him," she said, "or rather he favors you, I should say."

"Really?" the King asked, lighting up at the thought. "He

was growing into quite a young man last I saw. And Verena? My daughter? Do you know her, too?"

"She is an amazing young woman," Shea said, with great admiration. Suddenly remembering her association with Royce of Nebosham, she measured her words carefully. "She's a lot like her mother."

"Liliana? You know my Liliana?"

"Yes," Shea said, rather uncomfortable with the familiarity with which he was speaking about the queen. Regardless of their relationship over the past season, she still knew her place. "The Queen is quite a ruler. She has worked hard to help keep the peace in the realm. It has been…difficult of late."

"Do tell," the King said. "We have plenty of time."

"Truly, Your Majesty, I'd love to stay and chat, but we really must be going."

"Going?" King Marco inquired. "*Where*, pray tell, are we going?"

"Your son awaits just outside the cavern. We smelled your food. He could not enter," she said, remembering the magic that kept him from coming in with her. And suddenly it dawned on her. "And you…cannot leave."

"I am afraid you are correct, my dear."

"What holds you here?"

King Marco sighed heavily. "The Dark Warrior of Erebos has imprisoned me here. I am no more able to leave this place than you are."

His words struck at her very core, but Shea refused to believe him. "But I was able to enter. Surely there is some way I will be able to leave this place." The very thought of never seeing Connor or Arn again sickened her.

196

"How is it that you were able to enter but Connor was not?"

Shea glanced behind her at the staff leaning against the wall. She hesitated, not wanting to tell all she knew. She had only just met King Marco and was somewhat suspicious by nature as her father had taught her. It was prudent not to reveal everything at once.

"Maybe I'm just lucky?" Shea teased, as she rose from her seat. It would be dark soon, and she needed to get back to Connor and Arn. "Let's see how lucky you are."

ဆ   ⌘

Connor and Arn had built a fire a short way from the mouth of the cave. Arn sat watch while Connor rested. The trip was wearing on the prince, and he looked to have aged ten years in the past half day.

Arn lamented sending Shea into the cave alone. He knew full well she was capable of taking care of herself, but she had been gone too long. The problem had now become that he was unsure of how to help her. He could not enter the cave nor could Connor.

He reached down to tend the fire, poking at the growing pile of embers with a stick. Hearing something, he looked up and smiled. Shea was coming out of the cave...with an older man on her arm. Startled, he jumped up, hand at the ready to grab his sword if need be, though she appeared to be in no danger. He ran to greet them.

Shea saw him and smiled as she and the man reached him. "King Marco of Oakhurst, may I present to you Arn of Ravensforge."

Arn sized the man up for a moment before bowing low. "Your Majesty," he said.

"Your Majesty," Shea continued, "Arn is also from the Guard of Ravensforge."

"Two of the Guard of Ravensforge? I am most fortunate and will be well cared for, I am certain."

"Where is Connor?" Shea asked, as Arn rose to his feet.

"Resting," Arn replied, with concern on his face. "He grows weaker."

"My son? My son is here?" the king asked excitedly. "I must see him at once!"

Arn leaned in to take the pot of stew from Shea. "Starting a collection, are we?" he asked quietly.

"I hadn't intended to but it looks to be so."

Arn opened the lid, breathed deeply and grinned, immediately setting about putting it on the coals to warm.

King Marco knelt beside Connor and gently shook him. "Connor, wake up."

Connor stirred but slept on. The king seemed surprised at his son's appearance. He looked up at Shea. "He is no older than you. Why does he appear to be middle-aged?"

Shea sat down. This could take awhile. "The portal that leads to the human realm was destroyed in our escape. When Connor came searching for the Princesses of Ravensforge he traded the sword that King Beltran had presented to him to a one-eyed troll in exchange for the troll sending him to where they had gone. He –"

"*Molan?*" the king bellowed. "He went to *Molan?*"

Taken aback by the outburst, Shea and Arn watched, dumbfounded.

Connor awoke, rubbing his eyes as he looked around at

them, first seeing Shea, then Arn, then King Marco. He rubbed them again. "Am I dead?" he asked, in all seriousness.

King Marco spoke gently but firmly. "You may be, once I am finished with you."

Connor rose, staring in disbelief at the man before him.

"Father?" Connor asked, rubbing his eyes for yet a third time. "Shea? I do not understand."

"I found him in the cave," Shea answered. "He makes a pretty mean stew, too."

"My father doesn't cook."

"A necessary evil, I'm afraid," the king replied, as he stepped closer to his son.

King Marco embraced his son, and Connor, still shell-shocked, just stood there. Finally, after a moment of indecision, he wrapped his arms around his father. The king released him, holding him at arm's length. "Let me look at you," he said.

Connor sized him up. "You look different. Old."

King Marco raised an eyebrow. "So do you. You went to see Molan?"

Shea and Arn exchanged confused glances. "Who is Molan?" Arn asked.

"The one-eyed troll," Marco answered.

"How do you know of him?" Connor questioned, his eyes narrowing slightly.

"Good intel," his father replied. "An associate of mine knows him quite well."

"Who?" Connor asked.

King Marco's tone was grim. "Arak, Dark Wizard of Erebos."

"Who?" Shea echoed, suddenly on guard and unsure if the

king could be trusted. They would have to take care in what they shared with him. He could be compromised or under the control of the Dark Warrior. That was a chance they couldn't afford to take. However, Shea also knew he might have information that would be useful in their search for the Dragon's Keep.

"Arak, the Dark Wizard of Erebos," the king repeated. "He is to blame for all that has befallen the fae of Ravensforge and to some extent, the Kingdom of Erebos."

"How do you know this wizard?" Arn asked, his suspicion growing as the king spoke. He looked at Shea, indecision written all over his face concerning the trustworthiness of their newest royal charge.

King Marco sighed. "I met him once," he said wistfully. "The Dark Warrior, too."

Shea was floored. "You met the Dark Warrior and lived? How were you able to do this?"

"Come, have some stew, and I will tell you the story."

CHAPTER 27

The four weary travelers sat around the small fire and finished off what was left of the stew. Their stomachs satisfied, they settled in for the rest of the evening and, as promised, King Marco shared what he knew.

"Connor, what has your mother told you about my disappearance?" his father asked him.

"Nothing much, really. She keeps that to herself mostly."

Marco smiled. "It appears she has raised you well."

"Yes, well, she had some help," Connor said, thinking of Arland's guidance in his father's absence. He decided to leave it at that for now.

"Everything she has done, right up until my disappearance, was done with purpose, for a reason. She had to find a way to preserve herself and our kingdom. Certain things had to be done."

"Like what?" Shea asked, between the last bites of stew.

The King stared at the flames, hedging on offering a response to her question. "Love and duty, honor and sacrifice, these are the full measure of the worth of any good king or queen. Liliana knows this well – taught it to me, in fact – and she always made those choices with the good of the kingdom foremost in her thoughts."

King Marco sighed. "She was beautiful," he said of the memory.

"She still is," Connor said, "only older."

"Yes, well, I guess we all are," King Marco chuckled knowingly. "The Guardian to King Isakaar thought her beautiful, too."

"King Isakaar? I've never heard of him," Shea said.

"Nor have I," Arn agreed.

"Erebos was not always the dark palace it is now. It was a beautiful place to live, filled with many fae. King Isakaar was a good king, wise and kind, but very shortsighted, I'm afraid."

"How so?" Connor asked.

"He saw an opportunity to raise Erebos' stature and power in the realm, and it turned on him and bit him. He chose to elevate one whom he trusted with his life, his Guardian, to royal status after he learned of the powers he had gained."

"What kind of powers?" Arn asked.

"His Guardian became well-versed in the dark magic and provided Isakaar with unmatched protection and power within the realm. But the power corrupted this Guardian, made him arrogant and demanding. And, he had his eye on a princess from another kingdom. Believing he was of proper status to court her, he made his intentions known to her. She rejected him out of hand, and he was certainly not used to being told no."

"But that would have never worked," Connor said without hesitation. "She had a kingdom to rule. She would have needed to marry within her station."

Shea lowered her eyes and poked at the embers with the stick again, unsure if Connor even realized what he had said. Everything they had together had just been reduced to a painful contradiction with a handful of words. Worst of all, as she watched him in the moments following, she was certain he didn't even recognize that he'd done it. Perhaps this would make the task assigned to her by the queen a little easier when the time came.

"It was of no consequence," the king replied with a smile. "She had already chosen another."

CHAPTER 28

Shea slept fitfully that night. Arn had taken first watch as the rest of them made an attempt at sleep. Drifting in and out of sleep, it became difficult for Shea to distinguish between her sleeping and waking thoughts.

She found herself in a beautiful meadow surrounded by flowers of all kinds. It was even more beautiful than the gardens of Oakhurst, and she took in their soothing fragrance. The sun was shining and she felt at peace here.

"Hello, Shea," came a familiar voice from behind her. Startled, she turned to find Elisabeth smiling at her.

She was different than she had appeared as she departed Oakhurst. A young woman, she was vibrant, and her eyes smiled at her friend. She was dressed in light-colored pants and a white shirt, as if she'd just returned from an archaeological dig in Egypt of the human realm. So relieved to see her again, Shea grabbed her and hugged her tight.

"Elisabeth! Oh, how I've missed you!" she cried. "It is so good to see you!"

"Welcome back to the fae realm, my friend," Elisabeth said, as she took a step back.

Sudden sadness washed over Shea's face. "Oh, Elisabeth," she sighed. "I'm afraid I've made a mess of things."

"How so?"

"King Rogan believes I am not fit to hold the Relics of the Dragon Triad," Shea said, remembering her last evening at Oakhurst, "and I'm afraid he may be right. The Keeper of Time has been stolen."

"This is a problem," Elisabeth replied. "Do you still possess the staff? And the amulet?"

"Yes," Shea answered. "Molan the troll came to Oakhurst and took the relic. That is how Connor and I returned here. We were pulled through the ice."

"Time is of the essence," Elisabeth told her. "Connor will not last long in this realm. Molan sent him to the human realm using dark magic. Connor returned through the same kind of magic. He is aging?"

"Yes. Very rapidly."

"He will continue to age at the rate he would in the human realm. In the time you have been here, twenty years have passed at Oakhurst."

"Twenty years? But we have been here only a short while. This is why he was never to return home?"

"Yes," Elisabeth sighed. "The dark magic remains from his passage to Oakhurst. He was not supposed to come through with you."

Shea shuddered as she thought back to being pulled under

the ice by the portal Molan had opened up. "It couldn't be helped. He was trying to save me."

"And now you must save him. Just remember, Shea, all is not as it seems."

"What do you mean?"

"You're next up on watch, that's what I mean."

"What? Elisabeth, I –" Shea opened her eyes as she awakened from the dream to find Arn kneeling next to her.

"Who is Elisabeth?" he asked her, as he settled down near the fire.

"A friend," Shea answered slowly. "She was trying to tell me something."

"Was it important?"

"Perhaps."

ॐ   ॐ

Morning came uneventfully, and Shea and the others prepared to break camp. They had very little to speak of in terms of gear. She and Arn carefully stowed it for travel as King Marco headed toward a nearby pond to refresh himself. Though they had a good way to go, she could almost feel the growing darkness of Erebos upon the countryside.

Feeling some guilt as to whether or not Arn should continue on with them, she determined in rather short order that she was glad to have him with them if for no other reason than she had previously thought him lost to her.

And though Shea did not want to risk the chance of losing him again, she knew Arn would never let her leave him behind.

ॐ   ॐ

Verena's steps slowed as she reached a window bound by large boulders jutting skyward. Though they appeared to her to be poking outward as if from a wall into another room, she had a clear view of the sky above and the stone outcropping that reached toward it.

"What is this place?" she whispered, peering into the window as she drew near. A sudden movement caught her eye, and for a moment she felt as if she needed to hide.

Feeling a bit foolish, she peered around the edge of the window to see a man dressed in royal robes nearing. He knelt at the water's edge to refresh himself. Though his face was somewhat scruffy and unkempt, she thought him familiar. A quizzical look crossed her face as her mind raced to put it all together.

Suddenly, realizing who was on the other side of the window, Verena turned pale as if she'd seen a ghost.

On the other side of the water window, staring back at her, was her father!

ଞ   ଔ

Kneeling at the water's edge, King Marco splashed the cool water upon his face. He looked haggard, like sleeping on the ground was the last thing he preferred to do. Still, he had been nothing less than the "perfect" traveling companion and planned to keep it so for the time being.

He leaned back on his heels, taking in the view across the lake. Though not very big, it was beautiful and remote. Peaceful. Were it not for the task at hand, he thought it a good place to remain awhile.

The task at hand...

Things had grown complicated at best, and he did not know how much longer it would all hold out. *Just a little longer.*

A slight ripple a mere arm's length out caught his attention, and he looked into the water expecting to see a fish. What he saw next shocked him.

Staring back at him from beneath the water's surface was the beautiful face of a young woman!

›‼ ‽‹

The realization hit Verena with full force, knocking the wind out of her. She was staring into the face of her father! Gone all this time he looked older, yet still the eyes were the same kind eyes she remembered as a child.

Filled with joy, tears welled up in her eyes.

"Father!" she cried. "Father! Here I am!" Tentatively, Verena reached her hand toward the window.

›‼ ‽‹

From the other side King Marco could hear a voice, familiar yet so far away. He could see the woman's face and neared the water's surface with his own face as he looked closer at her.

He could see her clearly now, looking her square in the eyes, and he knew that she could see him as well. His mind processed the voice, and as it registered as his daughter's, something unexpected happened.

The king took his hands, wiped his face dry and with his eyes still locked on Verena's, stood and walked away.

209

"**Father?** *Father, NO!* Wait! Come back!" Verena begged at the top of her lungs. What was wrong with him?! He had seen her through the window – *she knew he had!*

"Come back," she whimpered. *"Please, don't go."*

Exasperated, Verena allowed her hand to rest upon the window. Immediately it poked through the water's surface on the other side in the faerie realm.

Verena's hand reached skyward as the king walked away without looking back.

ᴔ   ᴃ

Connor took longer than usual to get moving that morning as they set off on the last leg of their journey to Erebos. Shea watched as his movements became slower and more deliberate over the past few days. It was like the time lapse photography they'd seen at Sam's house on Thanksgiving Day. The production crew had filmed an entire football game from start to finish, then accelerated it to be shown in a span of less than two minutes.

And though Connor's movements were not accelerated, his rate of aging was. This particular morning they awoke to find he had silver streaks in the hair around his temples.

Wisdom, Shea had told him, but he didn't seem to appreciate it much.

Arn and King Marco came to Shea as she watched Connor.

"King Marco knows of something that may help him," Arn said, nodding in Connor's direction.

"Anything," Shea said absently. "He can't stand to be this

210

way. This is not who he is."

"The answer," Marco said quietly, "lies in Erebos."

Arn and Shea both looked at him in shock and disbelief.

"You're kidding, right?" Shea asked. "What can be of help to him there?"

"It is said that there is a room filled with magical potions and charms and such," Marco said. "Perhaps the answer lies there."

"That's all fine, well and good, but how do we know which one we need or how to make it work? Surely they're not labeled." Arn took on a mocking tone as he pretended to hold up various and sundry invisible objects. "Oh, *look*, this one's for making one taller! And this one will make you more handsome....*oh, won't* that *work nicely on imps and trolls!* And let's see, what's in this lovely bottle?" He turned, looking sharply at the king. "Surely you *jest!*"

Arn's tone caught Connor's attention.

Shea stood there, brows raised, stunned by his insolent outburst. Perhaps she'd misjudged him. At any rate, it looked as if the pressure of returning to Erebos was starting to wear on him.

"Arn," she said quietly.

"Forgive me," he said. Then turning to King Marco, "Forgive me, Your Majesty." With nothing more to say, he headed toward the path.

"I am sorry, Your Highness," Shea apologized. "That is not like him. He suffered greatly in captivity, and I am sure that Erebos is the last place he wishes to go."

"If any of us had good sense," King Marco replied, "Erebos is the last place we would wish to go."

CHAPTER 29

Verena sat on the floor in front of the window with her head on her knees and sobbed for what seemed like days. She cursed Niwadi, cried for her father, and wished like hell that Royce were here with her.

Drying her eyes, she noticed that daylight had finally filtered in through the series of windows she had passed by during the night.

What Verena saw in the light absolutely horrified her.

She slapped her hand over her mouth to keep from screaming. Not since that day in the gardens had she been so utterly terrified as she watched the Gutiku as they were drawn into the magic box. Though it had been a relief to see them disappear inside, she could have never imagined this.

Frozen in a tangled snarl of bodies were Gutiku as far as the eye could see. Held in some sort of stasis, agony was apparent in their black, craggy faces. Their lanky limbs were intertwined with one another, forming a mish-mash sort of chain of bodies that stretched as far as Verena could see in either direction. She had been walking past them all this time and never even knew it!

Calming herself, she rose and stepped closer to look at them. Their eyes still had a faint glow to them, their teeth still bared and ready to strike. They looked fierce even in their motionlessness. She raised a hand as if to reach out and touch one of them but froze just short of it. Thinking better of it she withdrew her hand.

No sense in tempting fate, she told herself.

Picking up her pace she began to move along the ever-increasing chain of minions. At one point she began to run, though not sure why, other than for the simple act of reassuring herself that she could. Irrational fear was beginning to creep into the solitude of this place between the realms, and she grappled with the rising fear that she may very well be trapped there, alone, for a very long time should she not be able to find her way back home.

Sprinting along, the cape billowing out behind her, Verena began to notice something – the skies outside the water windows began to change, becoming almost…*recognizable*. Commanding her full attention she slowed, drawing herself nearer to a window that was looking upward at what remained of a castle. She gasped when she realized where she was.

"Ravensforge," Verena whispered, as she fought the urge to weep. Connor and Shea were not dead – they couldn't be. Surely she would know if her brother were truly gone. She vowed she would find them.

Making her way along the window she recognized the

moat across the back of the property. It had been for landscaping purposes rather than security and was filled with beautiful water lilies in spite of the ruin and destruction above them.

Unable to contain herself any longer, Verena placed her face in her hands and sobbed. How she longed to see her family again! She desperately wanted things to be back the way they had been a short time before. More than anything, she wanted Connor back home where he belonged, learning all he would need to know to be a good king like their father.

But none of that would happen. None of that would be possible now.

And Royce – dear, sweet, impossibly simple Royce – she wished him back with all her heart and felt for the first time that she might never see him again.

In this cold, lifeless place, Verena felt nothing but dead.

A shudder raced through her at the touch of something warm against her waist. Sensing nothing, she wheeled about ready to strike at whatever had taken hold of her.

What met her gaze shook her to her very center, and overcome with emotion, she did the only thing she could – she fainted dead away.

℞   ℛ

They walked most of the day in relative silence, each knowing of the impending darkness before them. What had started out as a dark place on the horizon grew as the day wore on until it was well within their sight. The black sky above the valley in which the palace sat colored their mood, filling them each with a different shade of dread.

215

Connor's progress was slow, and though he appeared to be the human equivalent of a man in his late sixties, he moved as if he were closer to a hundred. By late afternoon, he was nearly exhausted.

A steep ridge stood in their path. At the base of it ran a babbling brook. Connor knelt to get himself a drink then sat upon a rock at the water's edge.

Arn paused, catching his breath. "Well, we could go around it, but I fear it would add at least another day to our journey."

Looking to Connor as he sat resting, Shea agreed. "Arn, we don't have that kind of time, and Connor will not have the energy to do so."

"He's going to need some help," Arn said quietly. "We may have to carry him."

"Then so be it."

ജ   ങ

It was late in the day as the delegation from Hawksgate arrived at the palace of Oakhurst. A complete detachment of King Astor's Royal Guard escorted Caeden, Torin, Finn, and Tristan in on hawkback, and they lit in the top of the canopy just outside the palace.

Caeden spoke quietly with Slade, King Astor's advisor, as he led the procession into the palace. The fae in the corridors gawked at the strangers as they headed toward the throne room.

"We would like to see the queen," Caeden informed the regent, who nodded and disappeared into the throne room.

"So proper," Slade nodded approvingly.

"Yes, well," Caeden responded, "little is left but anarchy should we not adhere to decorum."

"Really," Tristan replied sarcastically.

Caeden shot him a look. Now was no time to let it all fall apart. He only hoped the queen would be willing to play along.

The regent returned and opened the door. "The queen will see you now."

"Thank you," Caeden said, forgetting himself for a moment before slipping back into his decoy persona. "That is all, regent."

"So polite," Slade quipped, looking to the others. "Good upbringing, no doubt."

"No doubt," Tristan echoed, rolling his eyes behind the prefect's back.

Caeden and the diplomat strode confidently into the throne room followed by Tristan, Torin, and Finn, who in turn were followed by a dozen of the Royal Guard of Hawksgate. Old habits die hard, and out of respect for the queen and her station, Caeden stopped well back from the throne.

"My Queen," he said with a low bow, "may I present to you Slade, Prefect to King Astor of Hawksgate."

"So formal," Slade noted. "Do you always greet your mother in such a manner? Do you not greet her with a kiss?"

"Your mother?" the queen inquired. "I beg your pardon, Prefect. Caeden, what is the meaning of this?"

His cover nearly blown, Caeden leaned in to speak quietly to Slade. "She's had trouble with her eyesight of late," he said in earnest. "I'll be right back."

Turning to face Queen Liliana, Caeden widened his eyes in an attempt get her attention. *"Mother,"* he crooned, "you

217

look well! How *are* you? I see your eyesight has not improved. Let me come closer." He approached the throne, his heart in his throat, knowing he would pay for this later.

Going up the steps to the throne he leaned in and kissed her on the cheek, then backed off slightly, blocking the prefect's view of her face.

"My eyesight is just fine," she whispered sharply. "What is the meaning of this?"

"They captured me and mistook me for Connor. They are willing to let us use the portal, but there is…protocol. They are sticklers for protocol."

The queen looked to Arland and nodded, then shot Caeden a sly smile. "As it should be, *my son.*"

He took her hand and knelt before her, placing his forehead on the back of her hand. He then rose and returned to Slade and escorted him before Queen Liliana.

"I bring you greetings from Astor, King of Hawksgate," Slade said, relishing the formality of the queen's court. "Your son has been a most delightful traveling companion."

"Yes," Queen Liliana agreed, looking to Caeden, "he can be *most* entertaining if given the opportunity."

‟ ‣

The darkness of Erebos hung in the distance as the foursome finally came over the top of the ridge. The valley below them would have been exceptional if it had any sense of normalcy to it at all. Instead what lie before them was a seemingly charred landscape, in varying tones of gray and black. Even from their vantage point, they could make out the tangle of blackened vines that wound around the trees and castle walls seeming to strangle any hope of life out of them.

"We make camp here," Arn said, turning away from the sight. "We must wait until nightfall."

Shea watched him for a moment before speaking. "Arn," she began, choosing her words carefully. "You do not have to go any further with us." She felt physically pained when she looked into his eyes. She could see the anxiety building in him at the mere sight of the place, and she had no desire to make him relive what he'd suffered through.

Arn sighed heavily. "I have seen worse things than you could ever imagine. If I would not wish what happened to me within those walls upon my worst enemy, what makes you think I would send you in there alone, Shea?"

Connor cleared his throat, reminding them he was still there, but Arn chose to ignore him.

"I just want you to know you don't have to do this if you don't want to," Shea tried to reassure him. "But your assistance will be most welcome."

Arn managed a half-hearted look of reassurance before setting out to gather firewood. The king helped Connor settle in then headed off to help Arn.

Shea made herself busy clearing away brush and setting up a small fire ring out of eyesight of the castle. A rocky outcropping afforded them a good deal of cover from the wind atop of the ridge and would allow them to rest while only having to defend from one side if necessary.

"Shea," Connor said softly, "I don't want you to do this."

The journey had worn on him, and Connor felt as old as he knew he must look. He could see it in her eyes that she was worried for him, that she felt guilty that he had been dragged into all this. Truth be told, however, he would rather be no other place than by her side, even if it were like this.

Shea continued to busy herself with the tasks at hand. "It has been settled," she answered back curtly. "It is going to happen."

"Shea, you *can't* do this."

"Do not tell me what I can and cannot do!" she snapped at him. "The Keeper of Time was stolen on my watch…from my home! You wouldn't be here in this predicament if it weren't for me. It is my responsibility to fix this. Do you want me to prove Rogan right? And if I'd only done what your mother had asked of me weeks ago, none of this –"

Shea's words halted abruptly, and she wished with all she had in her she could take them back, hoping that Connor's pseudo-aged hearing had not heard her. Unfortunately, he had not missed that part.

"What about my mother?' Connor asked quietly.

Shea's mind scrambled as she tried to think of a cover for herself and the queen without lying to him. That was one thing she had never done with him, and though she had struggled internally with keeping Queen Liliana's plan from him, she knew that regardless of how painful it would be for both of them, it was for the good of the Kingdom of Oakhurst.

"You mother had asked me again to reconsider on the relics," Shea told the half-truth. "I was stubborn and would not."

She walked over and sat down beside him. Behind his handsome, wrinkled face were the eyes of the young prince that she knew and cared for. He was brave and strong and adventurous, and she hated to see him like this. Worst of all, he hated it himself, and she could see it in his eyes.

"Shea, it's not your fault."

220

"Nonetheless, I know what I am charged to do. Without the Keeper of Time, Rogan will lead troops against your mother's palace. He will lay siege to it," she said, her eyes reflecting her pain at the thought, "and I cannot let that happen."

She paused for a moment considering how he must be feeling before she dealt the final blow.

"Besides, you have no say in this."

"I beg your pardon?" Connor had nearly lost his patience with the whole situation and could scarcely contain his growing anger. He looked old enough to be her father now and was starting to act like it. "I have every say in this. Matter of fact, *mine* is the only say in this that counts."

ᛒ   ᛏ

"So, Your Highness," Arn began, as he gathered up kindling for the fire, "how is it that you know Molan the troll?" He hoped the casualness of his tone would put the monarch at ease, a little off balance. Something didn't sit right with his story, and Arn was determined to find out just what it was.

King Marco sighed. "Molan was a friend to Arak. Arak was banished by the Dark Warrior when he discovered that Arak was in love with Princess Drea of Erebos. King Isakaar had promised her to the Dark Warrior in a power move."

"What happened?"

"The Dark Warrior had been spurned by Liliana of Oakhurst at the Council of Royals."

"Your wife?"

"Yes, my wife," the king smiled wistfully. "Full of fire,

that one. She had her eye on me, and we were set to wed. He was humiliated. The Dark Warrior grew angrier over time, and upon his return to Erebos accepted the king's offer of his daughter's hand in marriage. When he found out we were in love –"

"We?" Arn asked.

"They," Marco corrected himself. "My apologies. When you've been alone as long as I have, you often tend to insert yourself into the tale in order to be entertained." He gathered his thoughts along with a few twigs before continuing.

"When he discovered that the wizard had set his eye on Princess Drea, he banished him and killed her."

"Why did he not kill the wizard as well?"

"The wizard had taught the Dark Warrior all that he knew of dark magic, making him more powerful than any fae should ever be. Arak's arrogance turned out to be his downfall, I'm afraid. Fortunately for him, he kept one trick up his sleeve."

"And what was that?"

"How to kill another dark wizard."

ꙮ ꙮ

The sun was low in the sky as Queen Liliana and Slade of Hawksgate concluded their negotiations. It was learned through discussion that there had been problems with the portal, mostly with it malfunctioning with disastrous results, including the loss of several of King Thereon's advisors whom he had sent on a reconnaissance mission. For this reason, Astor's grandfather had ordered passage through it forbidden. Over the passing generations it had been carefully guarded yet neglected. And while it still gleamed as though it would operate properly, no one really knew for certain.

"King Astor will allow your passage, but disavows any culpability in the matter," Slade advised them.

"Understood," Queen Liliana acknowledged. She looked to Caeden. "We will discuss this matter further in private."

"As you wish, Mother," Caeden responded dutifully.

Slade smiled. "I will take my leave of you now," he told them. "There is a long journey ahead of us. Your Majesties, it has been a most delightful visit with your family. And Prince Connor, may you find what you seek through our portal."

ॐ　　　☙

Escorted by Queen Liliana's Guard, King Rogan and his advisors strode through the corridors of Oakhurst. Reaching the doors to the throne room, the regent blocked their way.

"I am sorry, King Rogan. The queen is holding court with foreign dignitaries. I am afraid you will have to return another time."

"Foreign dignitaries, eh?" King Rogan echoed. "From where?"

"The Kingdom of Hawksgate," the regent replied. "They have been here awhile, and the queen will not be available for further consultation."

"Well, we'll just see about *that*," Rogan responded. With that, he burst into the throne room unannounced.

Marching boldly toward the throne, he was stopped about halfway up by a pair of sentinels with rather large, ceremonial spears. Crossing them in his path, the king took heed and stopped. No matter, he spoke his piece from the center of the room.

"I see you have guests, Liliana," he bellowed.

Queen Liliana rolled her eyes. "What do you want, Rogan?" She shot Caeden a look that spoke volumes. Rogan was not one for subtleties and could blow the whole deal out of the water.

"Only to have a say in matters that concern us," Rogan answered back loudly.

"This does not concern you," Liliana shot back at him. Then to the sentinels, "Why is he in my throne room?"

The sentinels with their spears took hold of King Rogan and began to escort him from the room.

"And with that, I will take my leave as well," Slade said. "Queen Liliana, Prince Connor, it has been my pleasure."

Hearing this, King Rogan stopped dead in his tracks and wheeled about, nearly knocking the sentinels over. His eyes narrowed as he looked from Liliana to Caeden and back again. Their eyes locked and Liliana raised her eyebrows in a silent attempt to stay his words.

Unfortunately, her plea went unheeded.

"Prince Connor? *Prince Connor?!* Well, now, isn't that rich!" King Rogan laughed heartily. "Prefect, I'm afraid you've been had."

❧　　☙

Queen Liliana stood on the balcony outside her chambers looking out over the darkened city of Muncie. From her perch she could see over the glow of the community that stretched on and on in the darkness.

It had been bad enough that Connor had been taken from her, not once but twice, and it was more than she could bear.

224

But now Verena was missing, and any chance of utilizing the portal to aid in finding them had crumbled before her very eyes in the throne room. Rogan had seen to that, and it was as good as declaring war upon her kingdom.

Arland stood silently in the doorway.

"You've brought him?" she asked.

Arland nodded and moved aside, letting Caeden pass. The younger fae stood before her, head bowed in shame and fearful to speak.

"Caeden, look at me," she commanded him.

Slowly, he raised his chin and his eyes followed upward, meeting her gaze.

"I do not fault you for doing what you had to in order to gain Astor's trust," she said quietly.

"Your Majesty, it was not my intent for –"

The queen raised a hand, at once silencing him. Her grief was apparent on her face as she took a moment to compose herself before continuing in a low tone.

"My son is gone. I do not know where, nor if he will ever return. And now I discover that my daughter is missing. Oakhurst is on the verge of war with Nebosham and probably with Hawksgate as well, and I fear I cannot think clearly with these things on my mind."

Stunned, this was not at all what Caeden expected, and he stood for a moment in complete and utter silence. When she said nothing, he took the chance.

"What is it you wish of me, My Queen. Tell me what I can do to be of assistance. Anything," Caeden pleaded, "anything at all that you command of me, and I will make it so."

"I only ask the impossible of you, Caeden," the queen answered him. "I want you to find my children."

Though the stew Marco had shared with them the day before was little more than a pleasant memory, none of them felt hunger on this evening. The sun was just above the trees in the opposite direction of Erebos, making the sky above the palace all the more ominous.

The four of them sat in silence for quite some time. It was Arn who finally spoke.

"Your Majesty, forgive me," he said, looking up at the king, "can you tell me how it is you know of this Arak, Dark Wizard of Erebos? I spent time in the dungeon of Erebos, heard things. I do not recall hearing of him."

"He had been banished long before your arrival."

"Yes, but surely one of his stature and prowess would have been spoken of still."

"It was forbidden, I'm sure. One does not defeat an enemy of that magnitude without banning his memory as well as his presence in the kingdom."

"I am sure that is wise," Arn agreed. "And the troll, Molan?"

"Arak's apprentice. Nothing more than a hack, really," Marco lamented. "Oh, he wanted to practice the dark magic, but he only dabbled. He was a lousy student."

The last comment caught Shea's attention as Elisabeth's words came ringing back in her ear. *Just remember, Shea, all is not as it seems.*

Her eyes shot to Arn's. They had served together long enough for him to know exactly what she was thinking. He jumped to his feet, unsheathing his sword as he rose, the tip of his blade mere inches from the king's throat.

226

"Who are you?" Arn demanded, as Shea and Connor sprang to their feet. *"Get up!"*

"Arn, what is the meaning of this?" Connor asked sharply, as he steadied himself. He watched as his father also stood up, Arn's blade never far from his neck. "Is this really necessary?"

"He is not who he claims to be," Arn told them, looking first to Shea then to the prince. "Connor, even you have expressed your doubts. He is betrayed by his own words."

Marco's brows raised. "Is this true, Connor?"

Connor looked away, somewhat ashamed. "I *am* sorry. It has been too long, and you are only a fond memory from my past. I grew up without you."

The king bowed his head. "Then this is no longer necessary," he said, slipping the royal ring from his finger. "This belongs to you." He handed Connor the Royal Ring of Oakhurst.

Connor looked down at the ring that lay in his open palm. When he looked back up, his father was no longer there.

Startled, Shea drew her sword as she instinctually pushed Connor behind her.

The man standing before them was not King Marco of Oakhurst. He looked to be a bit younger, his shoulder-length hair somewhat disheveled and his face chiseled and unshaven. His dark eyes glistened in the firelight, and he stood before them, arms open, palms upward in a sign of submission.

"I am of no harm to you," he said quietly, "or I would have killed you as you slept."

Shea's eyes narrowed. She was feeling duped, and she didn't like it one bit.

"Who are you?" she demanded.

"I am Arak, Dark Wizard of Erebos."

"Then tell me, Arak of Erebos," Arn growled, "why I shouldn't drop you where you stand."

CHAPTER 30

"Molan did not speak of you," Arn said matter-of-factly to Arak across the fire.

"How do you know of Molan? Where did you –" Arak stopped, suddenly realizing where Arn had encountered Molan.

"They threw him in a cell with me. The Dark Warrior captured him after learning he had helped Connor reach the human realm. The Dark Warrior intended to capture Connor as well if the opportunity presented itself," Arn explained. "Molan helped me escape."

"And the sword?" Connor asked quietly. "Is that how you come to have the Sword of Nobility?"

"Molan gave it to me," Arn replied. "It was concealed in one of the pockets of his cloak."

"That's a pretty big pocket," Shea observed.

"A magical pocket," Arak said. "He did learn a thing or

two in spite of being a poor student."

"Molan is not one to give up something of value so easily," Connor added, "unless there's something in it for him."

"He speaks the truth," Arak agreed. "Though he was my friend, he does have his flaws, greed among the most prominent."

"Little remains of your friend," Shea said. "His one eye is black and soulless. And pretty creepy."

"The Dark Warrior has put him under a spell," Arak said. "His eyes are the same: black, void of light, seeing nothing and everything at the same time. If done properly, he will be able to see through Molan's eye as well as his own."

"Then he knows we're coming," Connor said.

"Yes," Arak confirmed, "he knows we are coming."

ಞ   ಚ

"Verena? Verena, wake up."

Verena awoke to a soft caress on her cheek. For a moment she thought she had awakened in her bed at Oakhurst. She nuzzled the hand for but a brief second before she sat bolt upright in complete and utter shock.

Next to her sat Prince Royce of Nebosham, looking hardly worse for wear in spite of all he'd been through a season ago. Verena blinked hard – twice – as she tried to wrap her mind around who she was truly seeing. Still sensing nothing, she sat puzzled.

"Royce?" she asked quizzically, somewhat dumbfounded. "Is it really you?"

"Well, I certainly expected a more jubilant greeting," he

chided her. "I'll bet even Connor would have done better than that, and he doesn't think much of me!"

"Oh, Royce, it is you!" Verena said, as she grabbed him and buried her face in his neck. The tears began anew and she felt a wave of relief wash over her. Gathering herself up, she held him at arm's length looking him over. "I thought I would never see you again."

"I'm glad you didn't think that way forever," he said. "Forever would be a long time to spend alone."

"Apparently you have friends," Verena said, glancing around skeptically.

"Not much for conversation, I'm afraid," he teased, "but they do make for lovely decorations. Do you think your mother would like a set for the palace?"

"Hardly," Verena replied. "They are not so frightening when they're frozen, but I can't help but think they're watching us."

"Yeah, it's the glow," he said. "Never really goes away."

"How have you managed here, all this time?"

Royce sighed heavily. "It has not been easy. More mind games than anything. It's easy to get a little wigged out in here," he answered. "And it has been incredibly lonely. I am so glad to see you!"

He hugged her tight again, holding her for a long moment. She pulled away and spoke in hushed tones as if they needed to hide their plans from the twisted army of Gutiku behind them.

The snarl of creatures stretched as far as the eye could see in either direction along the row of windows, and she shuddered. Remembering Niwadi's instructions, she smiled.

"I have come to take you out of this dreadful place," she

231

said softly. "Much has happened and your father is poised to wage war on my mother and our kingdom. If something is not done, the whole of Oakhurst and Nebosham will fall into shambles!"

"Then tell me what has caused this set of actions in my father," Royce said, "so that we might set him right together."

CHAPTER 31

Arak the Dark Wizard stood before them, caught in his deception. It would take all that he had and more for any of them to trust him again.

"You lied to us," Shea said flatly. She was angry down to her core, and it was difficult keeping it in her gut where it belonged. "Played on our sympathies."

"Necessary," the Wizard countered. "Would you have brought me out of the cave knowing who I was? Where I am from? With whom I am associated?"

"No," Arn shot back, "we would have left you there to rot."

"It would have been a very long process. The cave was a magical trap, a dungeon of sorts. The Dark Warrior created it especially for me, to torture me."

"Why?" Shea asked.

"Because he could not have what he wanted on several counts. He was angry, and he took it out on those around him."

"How were you able to take on the form of my father?" Connor asked. "And how did you get his ring?"

Arak sighed heavily, and the regret that lit in his eyes was real. "I am able to take on the form of those whose presence I am in when they pass on. With any tangible item that they had in their possession when they died – a piece of jewelry, clothing, their shoes – I am able to take on their form. I retain their memories, even if I do not take on their countenance."

"So you killed him and stole his ring?" Connor asked incredulously.

"No," the Wizard said flatly. "I did not kill your father."

"You were obviously there by your own admission," Shea said. "If you didn't, who did? And why?"

"The Dark Warrior of Erebos. Connor, your father stood in the way of the one thing the Warrior wanted."

"And what was that?"

"Your mother."

Connor cleared his throat. "My mother? What could she possibly have to do with the Dark Warrior of Erebos?"

"She is the one I spoke of, the one whom the Dark Warrior wished to court. When she rejected him out of hand, he grew angry. Upon discovering that your father was her choice above him, he began to plot King Marco's demise. It was quite some time before he was able to carry out his nefarious plan. You and your sister were but young children, and the Dark Warrior made certain that your father knew why he had been singled out for revenge."

"I was there…when he dispatched your father. His

234

thoughts and feelings, the very essence of him was impressed upon me in his passing." Arak sighed, his words heavy with regret. "It is a burden I carry to this day."

Connor and Shea stared in disbelief at Arak. It was Arn who finally spoke up. "Why should we believe you now?"

"At this point, I have nothing to hide."

ᛒ   ᚲ

"I am afraid your father is not pleased with how Shea is handling the Dragon Relics," Verena sighed, as she began her attempt to bring Royce up to speed on the situation.

"And he won't be until he has them in his possession," Royce conceded, "or at least one of them."

"The whole balance-of-power thing again?" Verena asked pointedly.

"Yes, but you have to admit, he does have a point."

"Yes, but he also has an agenda. The worst part is, he projects that agenda onto my mother and sees conspiracy where there is none."

Royce chuckled. "I think he just doesn't know how to handle your mother. He is, after all, a little out of practice and has not brushed up on chivalrous decorum and such in a good while. Now, if he were dealing with your father, it would be a totally different situation."

Verena stopped dead in her tracks.

"Royce, I saw my father," she said solemnly, as they stood before a water window that peered up into a beautiful canopy of trees that cast a calming green light where they stood.

"But your father has been gone since you were a child," Royce said, somewhat shocked as he took her hand. "How can that possibly be?"

It felt good to have him by her side once again, and she smiled up at him vowing silently to never let him go.

"I do not know. He was older than I remember. He was at the water's edge refreshing himself, which is very unlike him." Her brows knit together as she pondered his actions. That was not like her father at all. Something here didn't quite add up.

Verena paused to look out the nearest window. When she again turned to him, the pain in her eyes was more than evident.

"Royce, he looked at me – *looked right at me* – and did nothing. I swear to you, he knew I was here. I could see it in his eyes."

"Perhaps he is in yet another realm? The realm of the dead?"

Verena sighed. "Perhaps. Niwadi said this place is one between realms, so it may be that there are even more realms than those of human and fae."

"Niwadi?!" Royce said gleefully. *"You saw Niwadi?* How is she?"

"Oh-ho-ho, a *fireball*, that one," Verena chuckled, her eyes wide. "She said your father is none too fond of her."

"Father's treatment of her was, shall we say, less than cordial."

"Why?"

"Who knows. Perhaps he was taking his frustration with your mother's treatment of him in council out on her."

Verena felt her face flush. It was no secret that their respective parents thought little of one another, but it pained her to think her mother's disregard for Rogan would cause

236

prejudice toward another.

"They need to learn how to get along," she sighed.

"True."

Verena began again in the direction she had come from when she'd first entered the magic box. The windows were beginning to look unfamiliar again, and she merely glanced at most of them as they walked by.

Movement caught her eye, and Verena moved near to a window. The light was waning and from their vantage point she could see up the ridge above the window in the brook. Her eyes narrowed as she looked what appeared to be up. It was truly disorienting, as if she were lying flat on her back beneath the water and only capable of looking skyward.

"What is it?" Royce asked, stepping closer to the window.

"Did you see them?" Verena asked, hopeful it wasn't just this place that was getting to her. "I saw someone up there. For a moment there, I thought…"

"What?"

Verena sighed. "I thought I saw Shea."

"Shea? Here?" Royce asked in disbelief.

"Perhaps this is the realm of the dead," Verena reasoned.

"You mustn't think that," he told her.

"But what if it's true?" she asked. "What if we are looking into the realm of the dead?"

"Dead men don't age," Royce surmised. "Why would your father be older than he was unless he were not still alive."

Verena nodded in agreement. "It grows dark and will not get much easier to distinguish where we are, I'm afraid," she said.

"Then perhaps this is where we make our exit," Royce replied. "I am quite certain I've had enough of this place."

237

In the dimly lit quarters of the Royal Guard of Oakhurst, Caeden gathered his belongings. Freshly sharpened, he placed his sword in its sheath and strapped it around his waist, cinching it up and securing the strap. He reached up and took a fresh traveling cloak from the peg above his bed and wrapped it about his shoulders.

Turning to go he found Tristan, Finn, and Torin in the doorway.

"We heard what happened with the queen," Finn said, fishing a bit. "Has she turned you out?"

Torin glared at him and jabbed him in the ribs with his elbow.

"I have to go," Caeden told them, as he brushed past them. The less they knew of his mission the better off they would be in the end.

"Caeden," Tristan said, grabbing him by the shoulder, "it's not your fault."

"No matter," Caeden answered back.

"Rogan's an ass," Torin quipped. "All talk. He'll never wage the war he's talking up. He won't because he can't."

Caeden turned on him and snapped. "He can't but Astor can. Did you not see the power of the hawks? I have felt their might – *literally* – and it frightens me beyond belief. Remember the creature in the thicket and the horrible sounds? That was a hawk having its dinner. Do you want to subject our people to that?" He held Torin's gaze for a long moment. "I, for one, do not."

"None of us do, Caeden," Tristan said. "But what is it, exactly, that you think you're going to do on your own?"

"Fix this," he said. "I have to fix this."

"On your own?" Tristan repeated sharply.

"Not exactly," Caeden admitted. "I do need help. From the Guard of Hawksgate."

"Oh, *that's* rich," Finn laughed heartily. "After your little story blew up in your face today, you think you're going to get help from any of them? They'll string you up the moment you show your face!"

"Yes," Caeden answered. "Matter of fact, I'm counting on it."

Enter Erebos

CHAPTER 32

The Palace of Erebos loomed in the distance. It was massive, intimidating beyond measure. An enormous cascade of textured glass leaves framed in black steel, each staggered row overlapped the one beneath it. The glow from within was an unearthly blue that warned of the dangers inside its walls.

The travelers were silent as they pressed forward. And though none knew for certain what lie ahead, all knew that one way or another, it would end here.

The palace had no clear point of entry, no main gate to speak of. Somewhat stymied, Shea paused, glancing backward at the rest of them. It was Arn who stepped forward.

"This way," he whispered.

Shea hesitated. "Arn," she said, placing a hand on his arm. "I cannot ask you to go any further." The look on his face betrayed him, and she knew the anguish of his time there was rushing back upon him like a tidal wave, threatening to sweep him back away from her yet again.

"And I cannot ask you to go in there knowing what I know of what awaits you," he replied. He looked at Connor who was weary and had weakened further. "Besides, you need me."

Shea stopped and stared at him knowing he was right. Arn offered her a faint smile.

"How else are you going to know how to get in?"

ຂວ   ແ

"So how does this thing work again?" Royce asked.

"It's very simple, really," she told him, as she put her arms up under the cape and grabbed the edges of it. She spread her arms wide, opening them to show him the full expanse of the cape. "I wrap it around both of us, and we can exit the magic box."

"It doesn't look very big," he observed.

"Niwadi assured me it will be big enough for the both of us or anyone else we need to take through with us."

Royce glanced around them. "I don't think we want to take anyone else with us."

"Agreed."

"And we can just walk through any of the windows we choose?" he asked. Verena smiled and nodded.

"And we want to choose this one?" he asked, looking at the starry sky above the ridge where they had seen the fae travelers only a short time before.

"As good a place as any to start, I suppose."

Feeling somewhat giddy at the thought of leaving the place between the realms and its nasty tangle of Gutiku behind,

Verena twirled around. Not one for girlish actions, she surprised even herself and smiled as she came to a stop.

The cape wrapped around her then wrapped back about her the other way as gravity played on it. The blue orb she had carried in with her flew out of the inner pocket and hit the floor at a good roll. Startled, Verena went after it, stopping just short of picking it up.

It lay at the feet of the Gutiku.

Verena looked up to find the nearest of the nasty creatures glaring down at her, poised as if it might snatch the orb up. The feeling that they were being watched, that all eyes in the place were focused solely on her, suddenly washed over her as if the dam had broken and her sense of discernment had been restored. *Oh, how she wished it hadn't.*

Fear and anxiety threatened to sweep her away, and she knew that in order for them to escape she would have to keep her wits about her for just a little while longer. Resisting the urge to simply flee, she reached out and picked up the orb, her eyes never leaving those of the creature closest to her.

She raised up slowly and secured the orb back in its pocket.

"Come on, Royce," she said slowly, "let's get out of here."

Turning quickly on her heels Verena spun around and started toward Royce when something caught. She turned to find the hem of the cape snagged upon the claw of yet another of the monsters.

Panic stepped in and took over where Verena's ordered mind had once ruled. Frightened out of her wits, she screamed and flung herself at Royce. What came next terrified her greatly.

It was as if someone had thrown a switch and an electrical

245

current was running a huge series of lights that came on one right after the other. *The Gutiku were awakening!*

Horrified at the realization that the magic of the cape had somehow awakened the creatures, Verena did the only thing she could think to do. She reached out and grabbed Royce's hand.

"Run!"

⁖   ⁗

After a long climb up an adjacent slope, Arn led them to where he thought he remembered the entrance to be. "It should be nearby," he said, seeming somewhat frustrated at not being able to find its exact location. "I could have sworn –"

He continued to scan the slope, much to Shea's surprise.

"It's right there," she and Arak said in unison, pointing at the rather obvious wooden door in the mountainside. Looking surprised at one another, they realized it was the magic each of them possessed that allowed them to see it when others could not.

Connor pulled up short looking dazed and exhausted, and Shea knew they didn't have much time.

Somewhat perplexed, Arn reached the place the pair had indicated and reached out his hand. At once, the door was visible to him. Giving them a look, he pulled open the heavy door and peered into the darkness beyond it. "The passage goes in a good distance, then curves back around on itself. It should be unguarded."

"Why?" Connor inquired, slightly out of breath. "Where does it lead?"

Arn looked at Shea. "To the Pit."

Like Erebos itself, Shea had thought that tales of the Pit had been just that: stories told around the fires at night to frighten children, nothing more.

Apparently she'd been deceived.

"And what, exactly," Shea asked slowly, "is in the Pit?"

Arn's eyes were locked with hers. "You don't want to know."

৪ ೮8

Unable to dissuade them, Caeden once again found himself in the company of his three travelmates. The journey this time went much quicker since they knew where they were going.

"So what is your plan, exactly?" Finn asked Caeden as they neared the portal once again. "You wanting to get caught?"

"Not exactly," Caeden said, as he scanned the sky from just above the portal. He took care this time, making certain he took the long way down.

Reaching the portal, they looked about. Seeing nothing, they looked to Caeden.

"Now what?" Torin asked curtly. "Are we going through the portal?"

Caeden responded with silence which only further served to frustrate Torin. It was written all over his face.

"Patience," Tristan admonished him.

"Aswynn!" Caeden called out suddenly, startling those around him. *"Aswynn, are you there?"*

"Who the bloody hell is Aswynn?" Finn asked.

"You'll see."

As if on cue, a shadow appeared overhead. Caeden looked up determined not to be caught unaware this time. The four of them stood back to back in a desperate attempt to protect themselves. Movement overhead captured their attention and they watched as the bird circled slowly, moving ever lower with each revolution around them.

"This is your idea of a *good* idea?" Finn chided him.

"We'll soon find out," Caeden said.

Closer and closer the hawk came until it was within reach of them. The foursome braced themselves, each prepared to be snatched up and taken skyward and were surprised when it didn't happen.

The hawk swooped in near them and landed softly on the valley floor.

"You should not have returned," its rider said. "King Astor will not be pleased."

"King Astor does not need to know," Caeden said boldly.

"And why would I hide your return from my king?"

"What is your name, rider?" Caeden asked, ignoring the question he had yet to find a compelling answer to.

The rider looked warily at him. "Skyler."

Skyler watched them, the hawk beneath him prancing nervously as she sensed his apprehension with the strangers.

"Well, Skyler, we need your help."

"You lied to us," he said matter-of-factly to Caeden. "The king does not take kindly to liars."

"No, I'd imagine not. But as you may recall, I did not lie to you. Well, not exactly," Caeden reminded him. "*You* assumed I was Prince Connor. I never once said I was."

Skyler opened his mouth to protest, held it for a moment, then closed it, saying nothing.

"Now, Skyler," Caeden said, as he watched the realization of what he was implying come to light in the fae's face, "I have an idea. It's brilliant, really. Why don't we go to King Astor, and you can tell him I have returned. And then I can tell him who started this whole mess."

Skyler shifted nervously atop the hawk as the full realization of what Caeden's threat and its ramifications meant to his post and the preservation of his head.

"You wouldn't," he said.

"Oh, you watch me," Caeden threatened. "You have caused your beloved king a great deal of embarrassment today."

CHAPTER 33

The four travelers crept slowly along the passageway. Arn, who led the way, was the only one among them who truly knew what was yet to come, and he was especially trepidatious. Shea stayed close behind followed by the Wizard and Connor bringing up the rear. She was concerned about him. He had not felt like himself of late, and it was becoming more apparent as the days wore on. The Wizard's promise to help him once they were inside Castle Erebos was accepted by Shea with hope, but she still did not feel like she could trust him.

"How much further?" Shea asked Arn, leaning in closer behind him. Arn slowed as he neared a bend in the corridor raising a hand signaling the others to stop.

"We are here," he answered, cautiously peering around the stone wall into the room beyond. He retreated quickly, nearly knocking Shea to the floor. She managed to regain her balance without a word, taking care not to make a sound. Arn put a finger to his lips as he gestured with the other hand for everyone to crouch low to the ground.

"There are many beyond this point," he whispered. "We will have to take the long way around. It would appear something is up."

The foursome belly-crawled into the opening in the stone wall. What met them made Shea's stomach turn and her skin crawl. The phantom ache in her arm that bothered her on occasion had returned, and she recognized their adversaries in an instant.

Gutiku!

The room below was cavernous and bustling with the nasty creatures Shea remembered from that night in Oakhurst when she and Elisabeth fled the house through the tunnels. Only then they were much smaller. These were nearly half again as tall as Arn, and though they looked relatively the same as the smaller version, she knew they were even stronger in this realm.

She let her head drop as she brought her forehead to rest on the cool stone floor. "You have got to be kidding me," she sighed.

"You know of the Gutiku?" Arak asked, seeming somewhat surprised.

"They paid me a little visit at Oakhurst," Shea told him, raising her head.

Concern etched Arn's face as it was apparent he still remembered his encounter with them vividly on the night Ravensforge burned.

"Truly?" Arn asked. "I did not realize they could travel

between realms."

"Yes, but they were much smaller." Shea sighed heavily. "Being human does have its advantages."

"You said there is another way around?" Connor piped in.

Arn sighed. "Yes, but it will take us nearly half a day. We will have to wait until sundown for fear of detection and try again."

"There is another way," the Wizard added, "but I do not recommend it."

"Why?" Shea asked.

"It is the most dangerous place in the Kingdom of Erebos. Even more deadly than being in the throne room in the presence of the Dark Warrior."

"More deadly than the Dark Warrior? Oh, I hardly doubt that. What could be more dangerous than that?"

"The Queen of the Dragons," the Wizard answered. "We must travel through her nesting grounds."

ဆ   ဗ

Royce and Verena ran headlong into the growing darkness sandwiched between the row of windows and the column of awakening Gutiku. Though they were slow to revive and fully regain their dastardly strength and speed, Royce knew they didn't have long.

His mind raced as his eyes darted back and forth between the windows that flew by on one side and the growing threat of the creatures on the other. They would only have one chance, and he knew they'd better choose right.

Screeches and the clicking of claws on the stone floor behind them told Royce they were out of time. The monsters that had awakened first were now fully reanimated and were coming for them. He knew he could not remain inside the magic box a moment longer. It had been too long as it stood, and he would go mad if he lingered there, especially if he had to spend eternity dodging the Gutiku.

He looked over at Verena. Overcome by the sensations around her, he knew that she would be of no help and had to make a decision quickly. The horrific noises behind them drew closer, and Royce knew he had to choose.

"Time to leave, love," he told her, as they drew up to a window. In the darkness, torchlight above beckoned to them. Royce looked back to see the glowing eyes advancing in the darkness at an alarming rate. The column directly behind them began to stir.

Nearly catatonic with fright, Verena stood wide-eyed and helpless in front of him.

"I hope this works," he whispered, as he grabbed the edges of the cape and wrapped it around them both. It fit nicely with room for overlap as he wrapped his arms around her.

The pursuing Gutiku sprang at them, its claw catching the hem of the cape as Royce threw himself and Verena into the window. Uncertain what to expect, he took a deep breath and held onto Verena with all his might. He felt a slight catch, then a sense of buoyancy and relief as they bobbed to the surface of the water.

Royce released his grip on Verena out of necessity as they both began to tread water. The cape tangled about Verena's legs and she struggled to keep her head above the surface. Though unsure of how the magic of these windows worked, Royce thought it better for them to get out of the water sooner rather than later.

Reaching the side of the canal, he boosted Verena up and once she had reached the relative safety of the floor above him, he climbed out of the canal and lay down next to her, his lungs welcoming the hot, dank air.

ᔍ　　ᔈ

Walking shoulder to shoulder with the Wizard, Shea helped lead the way. The Dragon's Staff cast a soft light that gave them some warning as to which way to go. It wasn't much, but it beat stumbling along in the darkness. They could ill afford the light of a torch, and Shea had learned enough about the interaction between the staff and the amulet that never left her neck to be able to control the light issue. It was a mind thing, mostly, and she had gotten quite adept at making it work. Child's play, she knew, but it was a start.

She thought back to King Rogan's protests at the council meeting days before Enchanted Luminaria and their subsequent unplanned exit from the human realm through the ice. She was more than certain that he would be calling for her head and saying that the whole thing was a plot hatched by Connor and Liliana to secure sole possession of the Triad Relics. She did know that he was well aware that the Keeper of Time had been stolen but wasn't sure that even mattered at this point. All she knew for sure was that they needed to retrieve the third relic at all costs.

The Wizard paused at a juncture where the passageway broke off into two separate tunnels. "This way," he said. "That one leads through to the other side of the mountain. It has been sealed off from the other end for quite some time now."

"How much further?" Arn asked.

"We are almost there."

The Wizard eased his way along the ever-narrowing passageway in the near total darkness. Again, Shea had some command of the staff, but the light offered little comfort in the unknown terrain they were navigating.

They were crouching now, and if it got any smaller, they would be crawling. Shea wasn't sure she was up for that, remembering the last time she was in a cave. It had left a bad taste in her mouth. She didn't like being deceived, and though the Wizard seemed to be on their side, she had her doubts about him. Unfortunately, they had little choice but to trust him if they wanted to retrieve the Keeper of Time.

What was worse would be keeping the other relics out of the hands of the Dark Warrior. If they fell into his possession there would be no stopping him, and Shea swore never to let that happen.

"How much further?" Connor inquired, from the back of the pack.

"We are here," the Wizard said. He stopped at what seemed to be a dead end and leaned back against the wall behind him to rest a moment.

"What? This?" Arn demanded, pointing toward the smooth, round indentation in the wall before them. "What manner of trickery is this, Wizard? Or have you simply lost your mind?"

"Arn," Shea cautioned him.

"Maybe it was too much time in that other cave."

"Arn, that's *enough*." Shea was losing patience with him and knew they couldn't afford to delay any further. "Wizard, what do we do next?"

"Walk through the door, of course," the Wizard answered.

"But there is no –" Shea stopped herself mid-sentence, looking up behind the Wizard to see a beautiful, heavy wooden "—door."

It was ornately carved and had a substantial bronze doorknob and a small, decorative window above that. Shea noticed there was no keyhole. She stood up and tried the doorknob.

"It's locked," she said, standing up on tiptoes to peer through the window. A faint glow further down a narrow corridor told her they were close.

The Wizard rose and turned the doorknob. Its heavy tumblers clicked within the thick slabs of wood, and the hinges groaned in protest as the door swung toward them. "Not if you know the right people," he smiled at her. Turning, he stepped through the door and the others followed.

"Perhaps we should leave it open," Arn suggested, "in case we need to come back this way in a hurry?"

"I am afraid we cannot," the Wizard replied. "To do so would be most unwise."

"And why is that?" Connor asked.

"The door was locked for a reason – to keep something terrible inside. Do you wish for it to escape?"

"No. What could be so terrible?" Connor shot back, the exhaustion starting to get to him. "It's not like there's much worse than the Gutiku, and we fought them off just fine."

"This one is not of the 'just fine' variety."

"Oh?" Connor retorted.

"This one is different," Arak said.

"How so?"

"Pray you never find out."

257

CHAPTER 34

"**Where are we?**" Verena asked softly, as she lie on the stone floor. Though it had not yet grown unpleasant, she was surprised at the heat of the place they had landed.

Still on his back, his chest heaving as he sucked in the moist, warm air, Royce raised up on his elbows and looked around.

"I am uncertain," he answered between breaths, "but at least we have light."

"A definite plus," Verena replied, as she sat up. She began to remove the cape, then thought better of it. Looking down she saw the corner that had been torn off by their pursuers. Fear gripped her at the thought of the creatures coming through the water after them. "You don't suppose…"

Royce looked at the torn garment. "Well, it'll take them some time to figure it out, I'd wager. They don't appear to be the most intelligent creatures in the realm."

"But if they discover it will cover all of them – even a few of them – and decide to follow…" Verena looked fearful yet much more in control than she had just before their escape.

"Right, well," Royce said. "Better get a move on, then."

ഌ   ങ

The passageway grew ever larger as the group made its way toward the glow beyond the mouth of the tunnel. A canal flowed in from an adjoining tunnel and into a pool within the center of the cavern.

The ceiling of the chamber towered over them, and light filtered down from a room above. There was a rather large, ornate grate directly overhead that cast a beautiful shadow upon the floor of the room.

Connor watched as first the Wizard, then Arn stepped into dimly-lit chamber. He could see variations in the darkness but couldn't quite make out what they were.

The Wizard raised his hand and all froze. It didn't take Connor long to see why.

In the darkness against the far wall of the main chamber lay a huge beast. It slept soundly, its body raising and lowering with each breath it took.

They crept along, backs against the wall, trying desperately to blend into it, hoping that the beast would continue in its peaceful slumber. Shea followed along behind Connor guiding him as they went, making sure he didn't lag back. And while he appreciated her attentiveness, he wished like hell it weren't necessary.

The journey had taken its toll on him, and though he

thought he had put on a good front, he knew his travel companions weren't buying into it. He felt as if he were a century old, and in spite of appearances, he knew that he would be dead by daybreak if they could not find what Arak sought.

CHAPTER 35

Arak peered around the corner. Surprisingly, the corridor was clear and he motioned for the others to follow. They hurried a short distance to a heavy door which Arak pushed at and seemed quite surprised when it opened.

Shea shot him a quizzical look.

"I used to keep it locked," Arak noted. "Perhaps with me gone, the Dark Warrior felt no need. All others in his service fear him and would not dare cross him."

Arn helped Connor in and sat him down on a chair near the middle of the room. The prince welcomed the rest, and he laid his head on the table next to him. He was weary from their journey, and as Shea watched him, she knew they were running out of time. His hair had grayed even further in the last half day, and his face was becoming wrinkled and ancient-looking.

The room was dark and appeared as though it had not been used in a rather long time. With a wave of his hand, the torches that lined the walls of the room lit themselves, and firelight bathed the workshop in a warm glow. Stacks of books lay on nearly every flat space in the room that wasn't taken up by bottles, jars, boxes and other unusual and rather frightening looking items. It looked like an unorganized hodge-podge of junk to Shea, and she wandered slowly about the room taking it all in.

Arak quickly went to shuffling through the shelves filled with various sundry items, most of which were covered in dust as if they had not been touched for a lifetime. Bottles and jars filled with glowing, exotic looking substances in spite of the layer of dust upon the outside, all were there waiting for the Dark Wizard's return. A collection of severed fae wings in a case on the wall gave Shea a chill and she watched Arak as he shuffled through his belongings.

"Arak, really?" she asked, nodding to the collection hanging on the wall.

"What?" he asked, barely glancing up before going back to his search. As the expression of shock upon her face registered with him, he looked back at her and the collection.

"Oh," he said. "Those aren't mine."

"What?" she shot back incredulously. "What do you mean they're not yours?"

"You forget, Shea, I have been gone a very long time. My workshop became his workshop. The Dark Warrior knows nearly everything I know of the dark magic.

Arak looked around the room at the disheveled belongings scattered about. "He has been searching for something."

"And what is that?" Arn inquired, from across the room

amidst a stack of old, dusty spell books.

"The answer to the one mystery that I failed to teach him. A prudent wizard does not reveal every secret, especially if it has the potential to put said wizard in the grave."

Arak went back to rummaging through the contents of an old wooden chest. An array of charms, cuffs, and various trinkets were emptied out onto the shelf next to him. He began to stuff a few items in the interior pockets of his cloak.

"We may need these for later," he noted absently to himself.

Shea marveled at the number of wares the Wizard stuffed into his pockets. At the rate he was going, the Dark Warrior would hear them coming from two corridors away because Arak's cloak was as fully stocked as a gypsy's cart.

A noise in the center of the room startled the trio, and they turned to find the Prince of Oakhurst in a crumpled heap upon the floor. Shea rushed to his side and knelt down beside him, carefully lifting his head and placing it in her lap.

"Connor, are you alright?"

His eyes glazed over and Connor became unconscious.

Shea looked up. "Arak, hurry," she pleaded. She hoped this worked. *It had to.*

"Found it," the Wizard called back in a quiet voice as he hurried across the room and knelt down beside Shea. He could see the fear in her eyes as he took Connor's hand and opened it up, placing the Talisman against his skin. It was a circle of black cast iron slightly smaller than Connor's palm with open scrollwork that kept it from being too weighty. Arak gently wrapped Connor's fingers around the object for him.

Relief washed over Shea as she watched Connor begin to regenerate. The old man before her faded back into the young man she'd grown to care greatly about these past few months. At last he opened his eyes.

"What took you so long?" he teased Shea with a weak smile.

"Oh, you know," she countered, as tears started down her cheeks, "I always seem to have a flair for the dramatic. Sam says so."

"How long before he can move?" Arn asked from above them.

"A few minutes," Arak told him. "We should be safe here for awhile."

"Where would the Dark Warrior place the Keeper relic?" Shea asked, her mind moving on to the next task at hand.

"A prize like that?" Arak scoffed. "In the throne room, of course."

"How far away is the throne room? Is it heavily guarded?" Arn asked.

"Not far and most likely."

"Then we need a plan to get in," Shea replied. "Connor, are you able to sit up."

"I think so," the prince replied. Arak and Shea helped him move to where he could lean against a cupboard nearby.

"Hide that Talisman somewhere on you," Arak told Connor.

"Somewhere I won't lose it?" Connor asked, his mind still a little addled.

"You'll know if you lose it," Arak said matter-of-factly. "You'll age right before our eyes and turn to dust within a matter of minutes."

Arak's bluntness startled the rest of them. "What? You want me to lie to the boy?"

Shea took the strip of golden fabric tied about her waist and ran it through the open design of the talisman. It had wrapped three times around her waist with plenty of extra to tie it off, and there was enough to wrap it once to hold the talisman in place and once to conceal it. She cinched the knot tight and left some hanging for good measure. Once she was convinced the piece was secured and well-hidden, she quit fussing over it.

Emotionally drained, she settled in beside Connor for a moment, allowing herself to rest. She set her mind to work on how to retrieve the Keeper and get them all out alive. It would be a shame to come all this way to save Connor just to see him die at the hands of the Dark Warrior of Erebos. Legend or not, she did not wish that fate on any of them.

Arak remained to observe Connor's progress and seemed pleased that he was reverting back to his old self rather quickly. "He should be ready to move shortly, but it will take some time," he noted.

Shea rose and made her way around the edge of the room pretending to look at the pieces in the workshop while observing her companions' movements. Arn had moved in to have a conversation with Arak, and Shea saw her chance.

In silence she slipped out the door and headed into the dimly-lit corridor alone.

ঙ৹   ৫৪

The silence of the throne room of Erebos made Shea's soul cringe as she crept through the doorway, taking care to keep close to the wall. The room was immense in its depth,

267

and the ceiling above soared to dizzying heights, capped with the same hammered blue glass of the palace exterior.

It would be daylight soon, and Shea knew they couldn't afford to wait any longer. If Arak was right, the Keeper of Time would be on display for all to see. She hoped he was right.

Shea stepped cautiously out away from the wall and approached the throne. It was massive and would be intimidating to any enemy of the kingdom. To the right of the throne was a pedestal upon which rested the item she sought.

Walking up toward the throne Shea stepped out onto an open grate in the floor. It was beautiful iron scrollwork. Several steps out onto the grate, she looked down. It was dark beneath her, and a warm breeze drafted upward toward her. She noted the faint smell of sulfur, much like they'd smelled coming into the castle. A chill ran down her spine in spite of the warm air as she remembered they would have to exit the castle the same way they had entered it.

Upon reaching the steps to the throne, she was greeted by the glowing eyes of the Keeper of Time. As it always did when the three relics were together, the fire opals came to light, as did the headpiece on the Dragon's Staff. Shea almost wished she could douse their glow but knew she had very little control over the pieces. The amulet beneath her breastplate resonated in response.

She wished she knew how to use them – how to control their power – perhaps then they might stand a chance against the Dark Warrior. But her inexperience with them and her distrust of Arak made them nothing more than spoils of war to be taken home and kept under lock and key.

Perhaps Rogan was right. Perhaps she was not capable of holding such power. And yet, King Beltran had entrusted the care of the amulet to her, the most powerful of all the relics, placing its safety above that of his own family.

Shea reached down and took the velveteen pouch she had borrowed from Arak's workshop out from under her belt. Carefully, she placed the relic inside, preventing the light from its eyes from giving her away, although the piece atop the staff still glowed.

Making a speedy retreat she went straight down the middle of the room, crossing the grate in the floor. She couldn't help but look down and could barely see the floor of the room below. Shea paused a moment. Eyes cast downward she could make out the shape of something in the dimly-lit room, but decided she didn't have the time or inclination to find out what it was. Moving on, she reminded herself that she would probably find out on their exit from the palace.

She did not look forward to that but knew the sooner they got out of there, the better off they would all be.

Her steps quickened as she moved toward the door and headed into the corridor. Behind her, large yellow eyes peered after her from beneath the iron scrollwork.

છ૦   ૦ઙ

From behind the throne a single black eye followed her progress across the grate and into the corridor. It was progressing as according to plan, and the Master would be pleased…

છ૦   ૦ઙ

"Well, it's about bloody time," Arn scolded Shea upon her return to the workshop. "I turn my back for one moment and you're off running about the place. What's the matter with you?"

"What are you, my mother?" Shea shot back. She knew he meant well, but she also knew he was right. "I got it. We must leave at once. Is Connor ready to travel?"

Her eyes moved to the center of the room where she'd left him. He was still sitting there looking the picture of health, but he had not moved.

"Almost," Arn responded, "though it may be a little slow going at first. Arak says he will regain his strength, it just might take longer than we have."

Shea walked to Connor and eased herself down beside him.

"Where have you been?" he asked pointedly. His voice was quiet, and she could tell he was still weak.

"Stopping a war for your mother," she answered, leaning her head back against the cupboard.

"She'll appreciate that," Connor croaked.

Shea nodded and closed her eyes. She breathed in deeply, exhaling slowly, a technique her father had taught her to clear her mind. It might have been relaxing, but she began to notice an odor she couldn't quite place. Familiar yet most foul, she sniffed at the air a bit.

"Arn, did you spill something?" she inquired, half joking, half serious.

"Wasn't me," he replied from in front of the nearby shelves, breathing in deeply. "*Aayyy!* What is that?"

"I know that smell," Arak remarked softly. "We are being watched."

Shea's eyes flew open at the realization of who it was.

"Molan," she hissed, trying desperately not to let her voice raise above a whisper. She looked up to find the source of the stench.

Peering around the edge of the slightly open door was the troll, Molan. His one good eye was still black and soulless, and his gaze momentarily locked with Shea's.

"Game's up," she said.

"Stop him!" Arak cried. He sprang to his feet and rushed the door with Arn hot on his heels.

Shea helped Connor to his feet. "We must move. Now," she commanded him. She grabbed the staff. It had grown even heavier in the short time they were in the workshop.

Unsteady at first, Connor's steps were more determined by the time they reached the doorway. Arn and Arak were already at the end of the corridor. They took the turn to the right heading straight for the throne room.

Connor and Shea had only taken a few steps out of the Wizard's workshop when Shea froze.

The sounds of the night in Oakhurst when the Gutiku destroyed the interior of the house echoed through the corridor. Screeching and snarling and the clicking of claws on the stone floor made Shea's blood run cold. They were bad at Oakhurst. They were much, much worse in the fae realm.

"Oh, Connor, we gotta go," she said, eyes wide as she guided her charge back in the opposite direction. *"Run."*

Connor stumbled, and it took all Shea had in her to keep them both from crashing to the floor. It was an awkward trot at first, but Connor's strength returned with each passing stride, and they raced headlong away from the horrifying sounds that were coming their way.

She nearly dropped the staff as they ran. Her hand ached from having to clench around it so hard. It was as if she were carrying over half her weight in a compact, unwieldy form.

Shea knew what the beasts were capable of from the night she'd fled Ravensforge. Their size alone would terrify even the bravest of fae. In her mind she could hear Arn's cries as they overcame him on that night. She struggled to keep her thoughts in the moment to avoid capture, but with each passing second she realized that would not be the case.

Her thoughts turned to Royce of Nebosham, and how the prince had battled with Gutiku in the human realm to save them all. Shea hoped it would not end that way for them.

Rounding the corner, Shea and Connor came to an abrupt halt. It appeared, after all, that it just might go that way for them as well.

ಶೊ   ೞ

"**Molan,** *stop!*" Arak demanded, as they gave chase down the corridor. The troll's speed surprised him. He'd never known Molan to move much faster than a trot, and there had never been a need for that on his part before.

The two fae picked up the pace, ran to another split in the corridor and hung a hard right. Suddenly, Arn stopped cold. A few steps behind him, Arak nearly ran him over.

Molan the troll stood in the middle of the passageway with a compliment of Gutiku that filled the space at least six deep.

Arak quickly reached into his cloak and pulled out a worn brass cuff trimmed in leather. Arn looked at him wide-eyed, knowing full well what the Gutiku were capable of.

"Arn, I *am* sorry," Arak whispered. With that, he slapped the cuff upon his wrist and disappeared.

At once the Gutiku were coming at Arn in an attempt to prevent his escape and locate Arak. In shock and disbelief that it had come to this yet again, Arn could only stand there and let them come.

CHAPTER 36

The three of them were dragged into the throne room. The Gutiku waited in the corridor, save the ten guards that escorted them before the throne followed by Molan. Arn hesitated when they reached the grate, and the Gutiku behind him shoved him forward, forcing them to walk the full length of it until they stood before the Dark Warrior of Erebos.

The guard to the front of them handed the Dark Warrior the pouch he had relieved Shea of upon their capture and bowed as he stepped back into formation. The Dark Warrior opened the pouch and removed the Keeper of Time from it. Immediately the eyes set to glowing again. He once again placed it on the pedestal Shea had taken it from earlier.

He was imposing in a way Shea would not have even been able to describe if she wanted to. She wanted to look to Arn, to see his assessment in his eyes, but found that she was like a bird caught in a snake's gaze and could not tear her eyes away from his.

The Dark Warrior of Erebos' deep brown eyes looked straight into them all. He rose from the throne and moved deliberately down the steps toward them, his black cape billowing out around him. His countenance was hypnotic as he approached, and they stood silent before him.

"Leave us," he commanded the guards, and they obeyed immediately. Only Molan remained.

"My Lord," he said, "Arak has returned."

Shea glanced at Arn and Connor, realizing for the first time that the Wizard was even missing. She had obviously had other things on her mind, a headcount being the least of them.

The Dark Warrior smiled. "Yes, I know. Do not be concerned. He will be along shortly."

ℬ   ℭ

At a dead run, Arak pulled up short just outside the throne room. The corridor was filled with Gutiku, and he silently wound his way around them, stepping just inside the doorway. From his vantage point he watched helplessly as Shea, Connor and Arn stood before the Dark Warrior of Erebos. Though he felt guilty at leaving Arn behind, he knew that had he not, they would all soon perish.

He would only have one shot – one opportunity to strike down his former student with the one weapon he had left in his bag of tricks: the knowledge of how to destroy another dark magician. He had found what he had been searching for the first time before Molan had interrupted them.

Molan, of course, would be another matter, but remained

the least of his worries.

Arn was inconsequential at this point. It was Shea and Connor who would take the brunt of the Dark Warrior's wrath. Shea for what she had done and Connor for nothing more than who he was.

The invisibility cuff still on his wrist, Arak made his way silently into the throne room. Moving along the inner wall, he reached the far end of the grate and moved in toward the captives taking care not to make a sound. He would wait as long as he could before taking action.

He knew he would only have one chance, and he would have to make it count.

ဆ　　ရ

Shea's arms ached as she held fast to the staff. Both hands wrapped firmly around it, she tried hard not to lean on it, but it was wearing on her. The amulet that hung from the chain beneath her breastplate began to feel as though it were a millstone about her neck. She was almost grateful not to have the Keeper of Time in her possession. Hard telling what he would do with it, or how the dragon would respond to the one who held all the relics and actually knew what to do with them.

"I have been waiting for you," the Dark Warrior said in a hushed tone as he stepped up to Shea. *He reminded her of someone...* "It seems we have a score to settle."

Shea's brows knit together, somewhat confused. "A score?"

"It would seem that you have killed my Messenger."

"Then your Messenger got what was coming to him," Arn

added without thinking, the memory of his captivity fresh in his mind.

The Dark Warrior turned on him and immediately Arn was reaching for his throat, gasping for air.

"How quickly you forget, Arn of Ravensforge," the Dark Warrior snarled, as Arn struggled under his invisible grip.

Connor moved at the attacker and was instantly frozen with the mere wave of the Dark Warrior's hand.

Shea stood motionless, unsure of how to respond. She was horrified at the power their adversary wielded at will, but felt helpless in spite of the powerful weapons in her possession.

Shea finally found her words. "What do you want?" she asked, knowing full well the answer.

The Dark Warrior turned sharply on her, releasing Arn and Connor simultaneously. Arn collapsed in a gasping heap on the floor of the chamber, and Connor moved in to offer assistance. The Warrior stepped over to Shea, standing mere inches from her. The closeness reminded her much of Pendragon and his lack of a grasp on the concept of personal boundaries. He towered over her; it took all she had in her not to step back.

"What do I want?" the Dark Warrior echoed mockingly. "What do I *want?*"

Shea stood before the Dark Warrior of Erebos, legend and myth at the same time, and felt as though she could collapse dead on the floor. Her arms ached from carrying the staff, and her shoulders felt as though the weight of the world were upon them, being dragged down by the incredible magnitude of the amulet around her neck. It glowed a brilliant red and orange as it had apparently reached its final destination. It's home. It's point of origin. It all began and ended in the Castle Erebos.

"It seems you were responsible for my brother's demise."

"*Your brother?*" Connor interjected, the shock apparent in his voice.

The Dark Warrior's laugh echoed in the cavernous chamber. "Do you not know who I am?"

The trio exchanged glances laced with confusion.

"I am Dante Pendragon," the Dark Warrior said. "The Messenger was my brother."

Stunned, it took Shea a moment before she found her voice. "Darius Pendragon was your brother?"

"You seem surprised."

"I – I just…" At a loss for words, Shea stood motionless, the weight of the staff and amulet pulling at her. It took all she had not to sit on the floor.

Dante Pendragon towered over her. Looking up at him, Shea found herself drowning in his eyes. Scarcely able to breathe, she found she couldn't look away though she desperately wanted to.

It was obvious by the look on Pendragon's face that he knew this, and he held her gaze a few moments longer before releasing her. It was as if she had been submerged in water and came up, gasping from the mental exhaustion of the encounter.

Dante turned his attention to Connor.

"Fine *prince*," he hissed. "You have come to see if I am truth or legend. Well, before you stands the truth, in all its wicked glory."

He stepped over to him, looking Connor up and down.

"How is your *mother?*"

"Quite well, thank you," Connor responded, with a note of sarcasm in spite of the gravity of the situation.

"Yes," he cooed, "I would imagine so. You favor her."

Connor looked perplexed at Pendragon's reaction to him, his mind racing as he tried to put it all together.

Pendragon's lips curled in a devious smile.

"I can see you have not put it all together yet," he told Connor, "but you will."

☜　☞

Unable to concentrate, Shea was barely managing to hold her own. Fatigued beyond anything she'd ever experienced, she was about to give up.

Suddenly she felt someone brush past her.

Don't turn around, came a familiar voice. *Say nothing.*

Arak placed his hand on her forearm where she should have been able to see him and was surprised when she couldn't. Recalling her training, she stood there stone-faced and motionless.

Shea sensed his voice rather than heard it and knew that Arak was the only chance of escape they would have.

We must strike at the right moment – together.

Shea dipped her chin slightly in acknowledgement, strengthening her grip on the staff. The sword would give her intentions away, and they would have only one opportunity.

Shea startled at the sudden movement before her, and her head snapped up in time to see Molan racing toward her. His one black eye glared past her – *through* her – as she braced herself for impact. At the last moment the troll dodged and made a leap at the air behind her.

A horrendous thud of more weight and bearing than just the troll hit the grate, and for a moment the troll seemed to be

280

doing nothing more than wrestling around with himself. Briefly pinned on his back on the grate, it was as if he was held down by a force greater than his own. Getting an arm free, Molan grabbed at the air and pulled.

In an instant the troll's efforts paid off. The invisibility cuff was clutched in his hand, and Arak the Wizard sat atop his chest in full view.

Arak punched Molan hard in the face, and the troll's head fell back upon the grate rendering him unconscious. The cuff fell from his hand just out of Arak's reach, and by the time he figured out he was without it, it was too late. Seeing no alternative, he rose and faced his former student.

"The great Wizard has returned," Pendragon said sarcastically, his eyebrows raised in mocking disbelief.

"Yes, well, I came to pick up a few things," Arak retorted, knowing nothing he could say would help their situation at this point. He stood there defenseless, breathing heavily from the struggle with his old friend.

Pendragon waved his hand, and at once the Wizard's cloak dropped to the floor, along with any hope of escape. With a nod the Gutiku were upon them at once, dragging Arak, Connor and Arn off to the dungeon.

CHAPTER 37

Connor followed in silence as the trio was led down the spiraling stairs of the tower into the bowels of Erebos. Arn was nearly catatonic as he walked what had become a familiar path to him during his time in this place.

Once on the block Connor looked into the darkened cells as they passed by. A gaze considered too long by those escorting them was met with a crack to the head with a rather long stick. The prince decided it best to keep his face forward and let his eyes wander slightly.

At one point he thought he recognized one or two of the captives as royals from Ravensforge, but thought it probably the light and stress of the situation playing mind tricks on him.

The minions ahead of them swung open the heavy steel bars, and those behind secured them with a hard shove that sent them sprawling onto the floor. The door clanged shut, and the tumbler turned locking them inside.

Connor watched as Arn slid back toward the wall, resting his head as his eyes closed.

"Now what?" Connor asked Arn, glancing around the cell. "We wait."

৪৩ ৩৪

"I must say, you have become more than a bit of a nuisance, Shea of Ravensforge."

Shea fought the urge to flee. She wanted nothing more than to put as much distance between herself and this horrible place and this evil presence as she could. But she knew that he would strike her down as soon as she moved.

Instead she stood resolute, staring directly into his massive chest. He was dressed in the royal robes of Erebos, a midnight blue so deep it nearly looked black in the dimly-lit throne room. Inside, Shea seethed, nearly sickened at the thought of what Dante had put Arn through, or what he would do to Connor.

"Where are they?" she demanded through clenched teeth. "What have you done with them?"

"Oh, they are quite valuable," Dante replied. "I have put them somewhere...*safe*."

Chin pointed down, Shea raised her eyes up at him menacingly, her tone matching her glare. "Know this, Pendragon: I dealt with your brother. I will deal accordingly with you also."

"Really?" Pendragon scoffed, in a voice just above a whisper. He reached down, crooking his finger under her chin and tilted her face upward until she had no choice but to look

284

squarely up at him.

He was even more imposing than Darius had been. His eyes were deep brown pools, and his stringy, jet-black hair hung down around his face. The collar of his robe was raised, making the angular features of his face even more pronounced. His breath was hot on her face, but she dared not flinch.

"I have dealt with far worse than you," Shea lied, "and I do not fear you."

Dante laughed. "You should, child. Oh, *you should*." He released her, stepping away. The Dragon Staff in his hand dimmed as he moved farther from her.

Shea took in a deep breath, grateful that he had merely moved away from her. It was as if he had sucked all the energy out of her while standing practically on top of her. In her mind she had already played out three scenarios of how this would end. All of them involved her sword, and none of them ended in her favor.

Her hand moved to her sword. With his back to her, she might be able to get in one good strike, at the very least bring him to his knees so that she might have a chance to finish him off. Shea reached across her body with her right hand, muscles in her arm taut as she began to slowly, silently, draw the sword from its sheath.

He stopped, as if he could see exactly what she was planning. "It will do you no good," he said, straightening himself before turning back to her. The smile in his voice mocked her only half as much as the smile on his face.

His brown eyes flashed with anger, turning at once black and soulless like that of Molan the troll. A chill ran down Shea's spine in his hellish, evil glare.

Mid-draw, Shea made a decision. She quickly pulled the sword from its sheath and rushed at him. All the anger at what he had done to Arn, what he had done to her family and kingdom, and what he planned to do with Connor and Arak, rose within her at once, taking her to the boiling point where she could no longer control it. Shea barely got three steps toward Dante before she froze in shock and disbelief.

She looked down at her hand on the hilt of the sword. It felt as if it were on fire! She cried out in pain from the heat and immediately dropped the sword. It clattered on the stone floor resting a foot or so away from her. Shea grabbed her wrist in anguish, expecting the worst, but immediately the pain stopped. She turned her hand over, looking at her perfect palm. Confused, she could only stand there as he came closer.

"Are you angry, Shea?" he taunted. "Well, we can't have that, now, can we?" Once again he stood over her. "Would you like to see how it ended for your father?"

Stunned, Shea looked up. *"What?"* she asked softly.

"I can show you anything," Dante said, "the past, the future, twenty minutes ago, a day from now – *anything*. Even the goings-on in the human realm. But we'll save that one for later."

Shea felt as if he'd hit her square in the chest. She could scarcely breathe, fearful of what he might show her. She was afraid of what her reaction might be, afraid that she would be powerless to stop it. And that scared her most of all.

"But first I'll need something from you…somethi close to your heart."

Without warning the Amulet of Fire raised before her face as if the breastplate from her armor wasn't even there. Unseen hands pulled on the chain, dragging Shea unwillingly by the neck ever closer to the Dark Warrior. She leaned back, lowering her center of gravity, but it was useless. The soles of her boots skittered across the steel grate toward him.

She looked around desperately for some source of help. There was no one else in the room save the body of the troll that lie only a short distance away.

"Come closer, Shea of Ravensforge, and see what I have in store for you."

ಬ ಲ

The cries of the Dark Warrior's captive in the throne room of Erebos echoed down to the chamber beneath the grate and throughout the lower catacombs. Her horror at what was revealed to her as truth was evident in her pained and mournful sobs.

Arak, Connor, and Arn stood in their cell helpless, as Shea's mind was laid bare at the mercy of Dante Pendragon. Unable to stand it any longer, Connor moved to the cell door resting his forehead on the bars as he faced the fact that there was nothing he could do to save her. He stood there for a moment in silence before backing off, grabbing the bars and shaking the door violently as he shouted out in sheer and utter frustration. His anger got the best of him, and he swung around throwing his back against the door in anguish.

"We have to do *something!*" Connor implored, as his companions stood there watching his outburst. *"Anything!"*

"Pray," Arn answered quietly, "that he kills her instead."

Connor was dumbfounded. Arn was like family to Shea and to hear such betrayal in his words cut Connor to the core.

"How can you say that?!" Connor raged at him.

In a fit of anger he tore across the short distance between them. Grabbing Arn by his tunic and slamming him up against the stone wall, Connor placed his forearm firmly across Arn's throat. Arak was on top of him in an instant pulling Connor backward in a futile attempt to keep him from injuring Arn. Connor went with him, swinging wildly as Arn just stood there.

Breathing heavily, Connor took a moment to compose himself, then shook off Arak's restraints. He watched in amazement as Arn stood there submissively letting his head fall back against the wall as he closed his eyes.

"She loves you, like you're her family," Connor snarled. "How can you possibly believe that she would be better off dead?"

When Arn again opened his eyes, Connor could see his own agony reflected in them.

"It is because she is my family," Arn said softly. "The most damage can be done through her mind. The Dragon's Keep will enable him to access time at will, and with all three relics in his possession, he commands time and is capable of traveling wherever and whenever it suits him, dragging her mind along with him."

Desperate for another answer, Connor looked to Arak.

"I am afraid he speaks the truth," Arak confirmed. "There is nothing we can do…for now."

Defeated, Connor hung his head and wept.

Arn watched helplessly as Connor dealt with his pain. He knew firsthand of the malicious ways of the Dark Warrior. But he also knew that Shea was strong, and if anyone could withstand this malevolent torment, it was her.

Shea of Ravensforge, Guardian of Oakhurst, lay in an unceremonious heap upon the grate in the throne room of Erebos. The Dark Warrior stood over her, satisfied with the result of his pernicious endeavors. She had unwillingly given up her most guarded secrets, including those of the one he sought to destroy. His vengeance had been a long time coming, and there would be no stopping the fury he would unleash upon his sworn enemy and her kingdom.

The best of it was that she wouldn't even see it coming. With her son and the Guardian of Oakhurst safely ensconced in the bowels of Erebos, he would see to the complete and utter destruction of the Kingdom of Oakhurst. *And Queen Liliana along with it.*

"I have no further need of you," he said to Shea.

She stirred slightly but could barely raise her head up off the grate. The iron scrollwork left red indentations deep in the flesh of her cheek. Exhausted, she could only lie there and wait for him to end it all.

With a wave of his hand, the grate in the floor disappeared completely and Shea plummeted into the blackness of the pit. She landed with a sickening crunch on the floor below. In an instant, the grate reappeared as if nothing had ever transpired.

Shea of Ravensforge, Guardian of Oakhurst, was gone.

CHAPTER 38

The Gardens of Oakhurst were lush and green under the spring evening sky. It had rained earlier in the evening, and the leaves on the trees took on a vivid yellow-green in the sunshine against the dark sky to the east where the storm had moved off.

The sky crackled with electricity such that the city of Muncie had never seen. It rippled outward amongst the darkening clouds as they rolled in and settled above the gardens. Suddenly, a bolt of lightning struck smack in the middle of the brick path in front of the Carriage House.

Dante Pendragon stood directly in the middle of a burned patch that scorched the bricks and singed the surrounding plant life. The smell of sulfur hung in the air, and it was if the devil himself had come to Oakhurst. In his left hand he held the Dragon's Staff. In a pouch hanging from his belt on his right side was the Keeper of Time. And hanging from a chain around his neck was the Amulet of Fire he had taken from Shea, Guardian of Oakhurst.

It had been easier than he had anticipated, really, almost disappointing. He had expected more of a challenge, more of a fight from this one whose name had grown in esteem and notoriety throughout the fae realm. From the ashes of Ravensforge came this so-called mighty warrior, but what Dante found was little more than a girl.

She would pay, and pay dearly, upon his return to Erebos should there be anything left of her. But the task at hand took priority on this evening.

The Dark Warrior lifted the staff high above his head, and grasping it at the bottom, began to swing it in a circular motion. Slowly at first, it grew in momentum, whipping the winds as it went. There was an unevenness to his stroke at first, but as the gusts whirled around him, the intensity increased and the wind currents became more fluid.

He smiled at the thought of what was to come. In moments it would all be over. Pity – it would be merciful, really. He wanted to watch them suffer. He wanted them to pay for what they'd done. He wanted nothing more than to watch *her* pay.

He would do away with the faeries of Oakhurst and the sprites of Nebosham, and then he would enslave the humans.

Yes, it would take time, but he had plenty of that.

He had all the time in the world.

The works of J. Wolf Scott

THE CHILDREN OF AUBERON SERIES

The Guardian of Oakhurst

The Embers of Ravensforge

Erebos Rising

The Secrets of Oakhurst

Midst the Dragon's Fire

Also by J. Wolf Scott

All are available on Amazon.com in paperback and for Kindle.

About the Author

J. Wolf Scott lives in the rural Midwest with her husband and two children, who indulge her habit of bringing her imaginary friends home with her. More of her work can be found at jwolfscott.com

69979084R00190

Made in the USA
San Bernardino, CA
23 February 2018